Praise for
Dorothy Gilman
and
The Tightrope Walker

"A very touching and memorable novel ...
should become a classic in its genre."
St. Louis Post-Dispatch

"Dorothy Gilman is one of those authors
that we would like to lock in a tower and
command to produce a novel at least every
three months. To get a new one is to become ecstatic, to finish it is to grieve, and
to wait for the next one is torment!"
Chattanooga Times

By Dorothy Gilman
Published by Fawcett Books:

UNCERTAIN VOYAGE
A NUN IN THE CLOSET
THE CLAIRVOYANT COUNTESS
THE TIGHTROPE WALKER
INCIDENT AT BADAMYÂ
CARAVAN
THE BELLS OF FREEDOM
THE MAZE IN THE HEART OF THE CASTLE
GIRL IN BUCKSKIN

The Mrs. Pollifax series
THE UNEXPECTED MRS. POLLIFAX
THE AMAZING MRS. POLLIFAX
THE ELUSIVE MRS. POLLIFAX
A PALM FOR MRS. POLLIFAX
MRS. POLLIFAX ON SAFARI
MRS. POLLIFAX ON THE CHINA STATION
MRS. POLLIFAX AND THE HONG KONG BUDDHA
MRS. POLLIFAX AND THE GOLDEN TRIANGLE
MRS. POLLIFAX AND THE WHIRLING DERVISH
MRS. POLLIFAX AND THE SECOND THIEF
MRS. POLLIFAX PURSUED
MRS. POLLIFAX AND THE LION KILLER

Nonfiction
A NEW KIND OF COUNTRY

THE TIGHTROPE WALKER

Dorothy Gilman

FAWCETT CREST • NEW YORK

Published by The Reader's Digest Association, Inc., 2006, by permission of Random House, Inc.

A Fawcett Book
Published by The Random House Publishing Group
Copyright © 1979 by Dorothy Gilman Butters

Fawcett is a registered trademark and the Fawcett colophon is a
trademark of Random House, Inc.

www.ballantinebooks.com

ISBN 0-449-21177-0

This edition published by arrangement with Doubleday & Company,
Inc.

First Fawcett Edition: June 1980
First Ballantine Books Edition: December 1983

OPM 33 32 31 30 29 28 27 26 25

to Pat Myrer
with love and thanks

PART I

The important thing is to carry the sun with you, inside of you at every moment, against the darkness. For there will be a great and terrifying darkness.

from: *The Maze in the Heart of the Castle*

1

Maybe everyone lives with terror every minute of every day and buries it, never stopping long enough to look. Or maybe it's just me. I'm speaking here of your ordinary basic terrors, like the meaning of life or what if there's no meaning at all, or what if somebody pushes the red-alert button, or the economy collapses and we turn into ravaging beasts fighting over food, not to mention the noises in an old house when boards creak and things go bump in the night. Sometimes I think we're all tightrope walkers suspended on a wire two thousand feet in the air, and so long as we never look down we're okay, but some of us lose momentum and look down for a second and are never quite the same again: we *know*.

That's why, when I found the note hidden in the old hurdy-gurdy, I didn't take it as a joke. I could smell the terror in the words even before I'd finished reading the first sentence: *They're going to kill me soon—in a few hours, I think—and somehow they'll arrange it so no one will ever guess I was murdered.*

But perhaps I'd better explain about the hurdy-gurdy and why at my age, which is twenty-two, I am not out in the world setting it on fire, figuratively speaking, or graduating from Wellesley or Bryn Mawr, or doing any of those normal upper-middle-class things, but instead own and tend the Ebbtide Shop, Treasures & Junk, Amelia Jones, Prop., 688 Fleet Street (not your best section of town).

Actually it's because I'm so free, a word I use loosely and not without irony. Due to circumstances I won't go into at the moment I have been quite alone in the world since I was eighteen, and with a rather strange childhood under my belt as well. When I was seventeen my father packed me off to a psychiatrist named Dr. Merivale. I think my father knew he was going to die soon and one day he looked across the room and saw me, really saw me—perhaps for the first time—and he thought, "Good God!" So off I went to Dr. Merivale, who was supposed to inject confidence and character into me in prescribed doses, three times a week, at forty-five dollars an hour, and a few months after I'd begun seeing Dr. Merivale my father went to the hospital with his last heart attack and died. He left a rather surprising amount of money, to be doled out to me month by month until I was twenty-one by the First National Bank downtown. I think he hoped that Dr. Merivale would assume some kind of responsibility for me.

I continued visiting Dr. Merivale for two years, at first out of sheer inertia, having nothing else in my life, but gradually I began to grow interested in what he was trying to do. Actually it was like going to college, except that while other girls were studying Jung and Freud out of textbooks in class I was collecting dreams for Dr. Merivale, learning the difference between super-ego and id, discovering that I came from a trauma-ridden family and that I was terrified of life. I crammed just like a student, reading books on psychology all day and half the night.

It had an effect: one day I looked in a full-length mirror and realized why nobody had ever noticed me: I shouldn't have noticed me, either, in an over-sized gray sweater with stretched sleeves and a gray skirt with a crooked hem. I went out and bought a pair of bellbottom slacks, which were in style at that time, and a bright pink shirt, and a pair of sandals. The bellbottoms swished when I walked, and I liked that; the next week I bought a white sweater and then a blue one. One day I accused Dr. Merivale of being a stuffed shirt—heady stuff! He was really very pleased with me after he'd recovered from the initial shock. I can't say I blossomed physically: I was still thin and freckle-faced, with straight brown hair, but inside I was coming to life. I could almost forgive my mother for hanging herself when I was eleven.

After the big house on Walnut Street was sold I moved into a boardinghouse—Dr. Merivale insisted I be among people—and fell into a very growth-oriented regime because I wanted to change as fast as possible. I set the alarm clock for eight, rose and did deep breathing exercises, then transcendental meditation for twenty minutes and after that half an hour of yoga followed by thirty minutes of Canadian Air Force calisthenics (aimed mostly, I have to confess, at increasing my bust

11

measurement). Sometimes it was almost noon before I had breakfast. And three times a week I went to Dr. Merivale, and I hung mottoes all over the walls of my room like "I am the master of my destiny and the captain of my soul."

But I still had nightmares every night.

It was at the boardinghouse that I met Calley Monahan, who had freckles, too. What struck me first about him was his great calmness. He couldn't have been older than thirty, he had a red beard and red hair and every evening after dinner he would remain behind at the table and peel an apple, slowly and very intently. I knew nothing about him except his name and that he played the guitar; sometimes I would hear him practicing in his room, which was above mine: sweet lonely songs like "Red River Valley" and "Where Have All the Flowers Gone?" After about three weeks we said hello when we met on the stairs—I was feeling quite daring by that time—and after a few more weeks I stopped going into a panic when he said "How are you?" and one evening after dinner we actually had a conversation. He wanted to know what I did in my room all day.

I rather incoherently stammered out an explanation—it didn't occur to me to dissemble—and he said, "So what does this doctor do for you?"

I said he was trying to free me.

"From what, and for what?" he asked pleasantly, looking up from his apple-peeling.

I turned scarlet, and then after a moment said defiantly, "Well, for one thing I've learned I have an IQ of 140 and that frees me from feeling stupid, which is the way I've felt all my life."

He looked at me for a long time, gravely, without amusement, which was merciful, and he seemed to be making up his mind about something. He said at last, quietly, "You'd better come and meet Amman Singh."

What's strange about this is that after he took me to meet Amman Singh that evening I never saw Calley Monahan again, which always reminds me of Jung's speculations about "meaningful coincidences" in our lives, because if it weren't for Calley Monahan I would never have met Amman Singh. I would probably have joined the typing class that Dr. Merivale kept urging on me, and I would certainly never have found the note in the hurdy-gurdy. Sometimes I ask myself, would anyone else have discovered it, and if they did would they have cared, or done anything about it and changed the lives of so many people?

It's things like this that comfort me when I feel frightened about life.

I was very nervous about going out for the evening with a young man, and quite unable to decide whether it was a date or not, so I compromised and wore the old gray sweater with the bellbottoms: half old life, half new. From somewhere Calley Monahan produced a motorcycle—I hadn't known he had *that*—and off we roared through the streets of the city with me hanging on for dear life. In spite of having lived all my life in Trafton I'd never visited Clancy Street before, or even seen it. It was in the oldest section of town, a narrow street lined with decaying old houses, funny little shops and a few stalls set out on the sidewalks. We parked in front of a grimy wooden house with a lopsided front porch, climbed five flights of stairs to a grimy hall and walked into Amman Singh's room.

The room was dim and not very clean and he was the oldest man I think I've ever seen, and yet.... His skin was the color of coffee and cream, with a network of fine lines crisscrossing it everywhere, not wrinkles

13

so much as lines like filigree lace. He glanced at me just once as we came in, and I saw that his eyes were black, really black, like ink or a raven's wing or a black pearl, and so soft, so luminous they seemed to melt all over his face. When he looked at me I felt something inside of me melt, too. He sat cross-legged on the floor like a Buddha in pajamas; several people were crouched uncomfortably around him talking a language I couldn't understand.

We sat down and waited. Being here struck me as weird and a little scary and yet I felt a sense of peacefulness flowing over me. It seemed to come from Amman Singh: his voice, for one thing, so soft, almost whispering as he replied to the others, and then of course those luminous kind eyes.... I felt he wasn't trying to please anyone, or demand anything, he was simply *there,* and the others adjusted themselves to hear him. It was about ten minutes before he turned to Calley and said, "You have brought a friend."

"Yes."

His eyes rested lightly on me. "We have been speaking of violence."

"Oh," I said.

"The violence inside us all, the angers, the negative thoughts, the resentments, and greeds."

I nodded politely.

He said in his soft, whispery voice, his eyes kind, "When you entered this room I felt your violence."

Now if there is one thing I felt I was *not* at that time it was violent. I was soft, malleable, shy and timid, and having doggedly visited Dr. Merivale for two years I determined to assert myself. I said indignantly—after all who *was* this creepy old man who looked like a high lama in *Lost Horizon*—"But I *don't* have violence in me, my psychiatrist is trying to *teach* anger to me, he says I don't want *enough* for myself."

14

Amman Singh listened with his head cocked like a bird and then he said in his soft, singsong voice, "Always . . . how blind we are to ourselves. . . ."

"How?" I gasped.

His eyes met mine and held them. "A tree may be bent by harsh winds," he said softly, "but it is no less beautiful than the tree that grows in a sheltered nook, and often it bears the richer fruit. In your desperate longing to be like others, to be like everyone else, you seek to destroy what may be a song one day."

I sat, astonished. Of course I understood him at once. What he said was true, of course it was true: I wanted above all else to be—well, normal, homogenized, pretty, popular, not lonely. I had accepted my longing as logical and sane, it was what Dr. Merivale wanted for me and it was what I wanted for myself. Now, suddenly, all my exercises and calisthenics and galvanizing mottoes looked like little straitjackets I'd cut out and made for myself. I couldn't decide whether this funny little man was hypnotizing me or waking me up from a long sleep, and it was terribly important to know: I sat staring at him, and then I stood up and walked out. I left without a word to either Calley or to Amman Singh, and I walked alone back to the boardinghouse, went into my room, closed the door and stayed there for two days. On the evening of the second day I suddenly burst out laughing.

The next morning I telephoned Dr. Merivale and told him that I wouldn't be coming in to see him for a while, and then I tore down all the mottoes from my wall and packed away all but a few of my books. I began to walk around town just looking at people and flowers and things. Sometimes I would stop in to see Amman Singh and he would make herb tea and we would sit very quietly and drink it. Once in a while, but rarely, he would tell me a story, but not often, because there

15

didn't seem any need for words between us. When he asked me what I was doing I said I was waiting, and he nodded.

And then one day, two blocks from Amman Singh's room, on the street that bisected it, I saw this merry-go-round horse in the window of a shop and I stopped, transfixed. I stared at its lines, at the rakish tilt of its bridled head, and a deep sense of pleasure lifted my heart and made it light and full of music. It was the first time in my life I'd felt an emotion that was all mine, and the first time I'd admired something not influenced or colored by someone else's words and tastes and thoughts.

I went into the shop, which was called the Ebbtide Shop, and I bought the merry-go-round horse from the gnarled little man inside. It was delivered to my room and I spent the loveliest week of my life regilding and painting the horse which I named—of course—Pegasus.

And incredibly, for that entire week I slept without a nightmare.

Unfortunately the next week there was a second merry-go-round horse in the window of the Ebbtide Shop—coal black this time, with a scarlet saddle—and since my room measured only 15 by 15 it was obvious that I couldn't buy this one, too. I went inside to admire it, though, and to explain to Mr. Georgerakis why I'd have to pass this one up. He said it didn't matter to him because his business was for sale, and a merry-go-round horse in the window was a good advertisement, and four in the basement was even better.

For the first time I became aware that I had turned twenty-one and had money. I asked him how much he was asking for his shop. He said he had a long-term lease on the building, which was high and narrow, with a two-room apartment upstairs, and in the basement

16

a storeroom and delivery platform. For the business itself he was asking twelve thousand dollars.

I bought the shop that same day: bought it lock, stock and barrel and without haggling. Its more valuable stock consisted of five merry-go-round horses, two player pianos, three antique dolls, a jukebox, piles of old clothes, and a hurdy-gurdy. I scrubbed and swept and painted, had a new sign made for outside, and hung blue-and-white-striped curtains on gold rings at the back of the window. What I could not do was discipline the overwhelming amount of junk that Mr. Georgerakis had bought in cases and cartons, and by the dozen; if I threw it out there'd be almost nothing left in the shop and so I cut prices and hoped it would move slowly and steadily out of the door in the hands of customers.

The hurdy-gurdy I didn't find until later, after I'd moved in upstairs, because it was covered with burlap and stood in a dark corner of the shop. It was a beautiful hurdy-gurdy, in mint condition for its age. It stood on a sturdy maple stick, and the strap for carrying it was only a little frayed. The box itself was glorious: a faded Chinese red with gold edging, and in the center was this bright, rather corny painting of towering blue alps, a river gorge and a cream-colored sky. Very Rousseau. When I turned the crank there was a creak, and then a twang, and the instrument actually began to play "Tales from the Vienna Woods." After that came a second tune: a faded slip of paper glued to the side told me that it was Sonata No. 1 from Vivaldi's "Il Pastor Fido," and this was followed by the "Blue Danube Waltz." I knew I couldn't part with this; I carried it upstairs to the apartment and began playing it evenings when I wasn't teaching myself how to play the banjo, or doing accounts.

One evening about three weeks later the hurdy-gurdy crank got stuck and refused to budge, silencing the "Blue Danube Waltz" on its second note. I found a screwdriver and pried open the back panel, which fitted loosely anyway, and that's when I discovered that a folded slip of paper had slowly worked its way down toward the working mechanism. It was this that had brought it to a halt. I carefully lifted out the wad of paper with a pair of eyebrow tweezers and tried the crank again. It moved smoothly, and the "Blue Danube Waltz" resumed playing at once. I screwed the panel back into place and only then noticed the slip of paper I'd tossed on the floor. I picked it up, smoothed it out to see what it might be, and met with a terror far worse than my own.

I read: *They're going to kill me soon—in a few hours I think—and somehow they'll arrange it so no one will ever guess I was murdered. Why did I sign that paper last night? I was so hungry and tired but this morning I knew I should never have signed it. Whatever it was it was my death warrant.*

But to die so strangely, a prisoner in my own house! WHY HASN'T SOMEONE COME? What have these two clever faceless ones told Nora, or even Robin, to explain my silence? Never mind, what has to be faced now is Death. Perhaps I could hide these words somewhere in a different place in the hope that one day someone will find them—that would make Death less lonely. And so—should anyone ever find this—my name is Hannah. . . .

The last letter collapsed under my eyes, the *h* ending in a long shaken stroke that dropped several inches below the line, as if the pen had slipped, as if a voice had been heard, or a step approaching. . . . I pictured this unknown Hannah trembling—as I was trembling now—folding up this paper, holding it a moment, wide-eyed as she looked around a room for a hiding-place, and then the quick move to the hurdy-gurdy with its loose back panel, and the slipping of it through the crack.

What kind of person would own a hurdy-gurdy? The paper on which the words were written was faded but it was the kind of cheap yellow paper you can buy in any stationery store, a ream of it for two or three dollars, called "seconds." Cheap yellow fades fast, so that didn't mean a great deal. The handwriting looked sensible, and it was certainly legible, even if the words ran together a little toward the end. There was that paragraph, too; I didn't think I would have bothered with a paragraph if I knew I was going to be murdered any minute. The handwriting was a little small but not cramped. What kind of person was this? I wanted to know. My wanting was so strong it astonished me.

Sometimes when I'm in a certain mood I've looked at life from a great distance, like peering at it through the small end of a pair of binoculars, and I wonder about it. The whole business seems very strange to me, just one shot at threescore years and ten, and for what? I mean, there has to be a reason for being here; even no reason is a reason. One of Amman Singh's stories is that we're on this planet because there are gods and demons in the universe who are numb to feeling, and so they send us here to watch our antics and feel violence through us, vicariously, because it's violence that feeds them and keeps them alive. And the only way to escape being "eaten," as he calls it, is to study violent emotions, detach oneself from them, and so cheat the gods and demons. Well, why not? People do seem to make such a botch of living: killing and squabbling and rejecting and hating, as if life's some kind of toy to play with or destroy. Somehow we all end up victims, and the horror of it is that we're victims of each other.

And now I was meeting another victim.

What kind of paper had they wanted her to sign?

19

She couldn't still be alive. The hurdy-gurdy had been mine for several weeks and before that it had belonged to Mr. Georgerakis.

This woman didn't know me, and I didn't know her, but she must have gone to her death thinking about me, taking comfort from the thought that she had left these words behind her and that someone would find them. It said so right here: "that would make Death less lonely." She wouldn't mean death itself, she would mean those frightening moments just before it happens, when a person feels nakedly alone and unknowing. She must have clung to the thought of me then as one last final hope, a small candle flame in her midnight.

How had they kidded her, these people she called the clever faceless ones? Had they really managed her death so that no one knew she'd been murdered?

Would that be possible?

I placed the piece of yellow paper on the table and walked into the kitchen and poured water into a pan and measured instant coffee into a mug. I felt really shaken, finding a thing like that in the hurdy-gurdy. The old clock on the shelf told me that it was half-past ten. It was so quiet in these two rooms over the shop that I could hear each tick, like a heart beating, and then a truck passed on the street outside and blurred the silence. The kitchen was very plain: oilcloth tacked to the wall behind the sink, and scruffy linoleum on the floor. No counter top but a long old wooden table with knife cuts on it, scrubbed clean; an ancient gas stove, two sets of homemade wooden shelves for groceries and dishes, and a really decadent refrigerator that snored peacefully for days and then suddenly vibrated wildly until I gave it a kick and put it to sleep again. The bath was off the short passage to the living room, and very much the same.

Coffee in hand I returned to the living room, carefully avoiding the slip of yellow paper that I could see waiting for me out of the corner of my eye. The coffee grounded me, it returned me to the present: so did Pegasus, standing guard next to my couch-bed, his head high and mane flying. I went to one of the two windows and opened it and looked out. The street was silent and empty but not dark; this was a street where other people lived over shops, too, the family across the street who ran the secondhand book store, the dressmaker next to them, the Nearly New Clothes Shop beyond, and the palmist, Madame Helen, above that. The lights were bright squares: one by one I watched them extinguished.

I thought, "There must be some way to find out who wrote that note."

"Don't be ridiculous," scoffed the contrary half of me, "it could have been written years ago. And she didn't even give her name."

"She gave half of it."

"You *think* she gave half of it. It could just as easily have been written by a man named Hannahsburg or some such."

"But the note was written, it doesn't matter by whom."

"Yes, and the person who wrote it is probably walking around alive and sound at this very minute. Don't be a fool."

"If she's alive, then why didn't she recover the note and tear it up?"

"Too much trouble, of course. The nightmare was over."

"I'm familiar with nightmares," I pointed out dryly, "and they are not ended so easily. She wouldn't have forgotten that note."

21

"Then if you believe she's dead, what's the point of trying to find out anything about her?"

"It's a responsibility."

"Don't be a fool. Dr. Merivale said you're much too imaginative, and don't forget that streak of the morbid in you. Next you'll be saying it's a hand reaching out to you from the grave."

"There's nothing gravelike about that letter," I argued. "I think she valued life, and I admire that. And she addressed the note to me. She wrote it to whoever found it and I found it, didn't I? And there's *no one else to care*."

"Then you just might tell me what you think you can do."

And of course I hadn't the slightest idea.

I turned from the window and looked at the room behind me. In this room I'd affected my environment, as Dr. Merivale would phrase it; he was always urging me to affect my environment. I'd sanded the bumpy old plaster walls and painted them off-white, and a man had come in with a machine to refinish the hardwood floor. It was a room that pleased me very much: there was Pegasus rearing up beside the couch, a Buffet print on the wall, a yellow beanbag chair, a thick rug in primary colors, a number of plants hanging from the ceiling in rope bags—and of course the hurdy-gurdy against the wall beside my banjo. This room was my cocoon now, its shining white walls and bright colors were what gave my downstairs life in the shop a lovely dimension. I didn't want to lose the sensuous delight of creating more of this—I hadn't even begun on the kitchen. I didn't want to turn my attention elsewhere, which I would have to do if I went plunging out into the world to look for a woman who had written that she was going to be murdered, and who was probably dead now, anyway. Where would a person begin if they decided to look?

I filled my garden sprayer with water and walked around absent-mindedly spraying my plants for the second time that day. After that I placed Rachmaninoff's Second Piano Concerto on the phonograph and lay on the floor and listened to it, and when that ended it was midnight and I fooled around a little with the banjo, plunking out "She'll Be Coming Round the Mountain," and "Little Maggie." Attention is a funny thing: when I meditate I can concentrate on an imaginary candle flame and reach a point where I see all kinds of lovely flashing lights on the periphery. That's what I was doing now, concentrating on the banjo and hoping I'd find something off on the side.

But already in the pit of my stomach I knew that I was going to do *something*. I had to, don't ask me why.

At two o'clock I turned off the light and climbed into bed and lay down, and then I got up and turned on the light again, and looked up two addresses in the phone book, one of them in the yellow pages. Feeling better, I set the alarm clock and returned to bed. I had expected to toss and turn, and frankly I'd expected a nightmare or two—at the very least that hand reaching up to me from the grave—but I slept soundly and serenely until the alarm woke me at seven.

2

Mr. Georgerakis met me with a scowl at the door of his apartment. He was wearing one of the Indian blanket bathrobes from the shop which he must have bought in volume years ago because there were still a dozen left, and the price changes on their tags were as long as a grocery receipt, moving from $12.99 to $2.00, all with artistic slashes. I can't say that the garish colors did much for Mr. Georgerakis' figure, which was shaped like a Chianti bottle, his considerable weight having dropped between his hips like a woman in the last month of pregnancy, leaving him a thin man at the top and a plump one at the bottom: it made for an interesting line.

He gave me a baleful stare. "I warned you business was slow, you can't tell me I deceived you."

I hurried to explain that I hadn't come to complain but to ask about the hurdy-gurdy, and by the time I'd finished explaining I realized I'd taken him much too seriously: he was looking amused, a twinkle in his eyes, as if he found me very funny. "Come in and sit," he said. "Sit and have a cup of coffee. You took the stairs too fast, you're too young for a fifth floor walkup. Only old men like me can manage such a climb."

"How do *you* manage it?" I asked.

"Slowly, like a climb up the Matterhorn. Sugar? Cream?"

"Black," I told him, "and thank you very much, Mr. Georgerakis."

He peered at me from under his heavy gray brows. "You're a very polite young woman, Miss Jones. Loosen up a little, you'll live longer."

"I'm trying," I told him.

"Try harder. Now what's this about the hurdy-gurdy?"

I'd worked out what I felt was a convincing little story. If politeness was my severest affliction at that time it was also, I'd found, a very good smokescreen for telling a lie. Nobody doubts anyone who's polite; it implies a tremendous respect for authority. I told him that a customer was very interested in buying the hurdy-gurdy but first wanted to learn its history from the original owner. "I'm hoping you can remember who you bought it from so I can trace it," I told him.

"Remember, no," he said.

Damn, I thought, and suddenly realized how much this had begun to mean to me.

"But look it up I can," he said, blowing into his cup of steaming coffee.

"Look it up?" I said dazedly. "You mean you have *records?*"

He gave me a reproachful glance. "These I offered to you at the lawyers' office. You should yourself keep records, because of the police. Sometimes things that people sell are hot, stolen, illegal."

I vaguely remembered his saying something about this. At the time it had seemed unlikely that anything in the shop was worth more of a fuss than the bathrobes marked down from $12.99 to $2.00, but I had been grateful for the names of the auction houses at which he'd found the merry-go-round horses, and had let it go at that. "Then do you mean there really is a possibility—?" My hopes, which had nose-dived, crawled up one rung of the ladder and hung there, waiting for his reply.

He shrugged his thin shoulders. "Maybe yes, maybe no." Getting to his feet he opened a door in the passageway to the front door and went into another room. I heard the murmur of a woman's voice, which surprised me because at the time I bought the shop from him he was definitely not married. Maybe he still wasn't; it gave Mr. Georgerakis a new and interesting facet.

A minute later he padded back, closing the door behind him and carrying a black notebook. "It was six, maybe eight months ago," he said, thumbing through the pages, and nodded. "You're in luck, sometimes a customer gets huffy about leaving a name, but this one I knew. One hurdy-gurdy, a hundred dollars, November nine . . . Oliver Keene—he's been in before, usually to sell me paintings when he's broke. Painter chap. Buys old costumes for his models, too, when he's in the chips. I don't know where he lives."

"Oliver Keene," I repeated. I took out the small spiral notebook I'd bought on the way and copied down the name, my heart beating faster at this triumph. I really felt pleased; I couldn't forget the horrified feeling that had struck me when I thought for that moment that Mr. Georgerakis couldn't help me. I said, "This is wonderful—I really appreciate it." Putting away my notebook I asked innocently, "You live alone here, Mr. Georgerakis?" After all, the hurdy-gurdy had been in his possession for six months and I wasn't taking any chances.

He rolled his eyes heavenward. "If I lived alone would I sell you my business? Of course not. For ten years I climb these five flights courting Katina. With twelve thousand dollars she marries me." His twinkle was back; he was really a funny man now that I understood his deadpan humor.

"That's very nice," I said, walking to the door with him. "I hope you and Mrs. Georgerakis will be very happy."

I thanked him again and left, heading at once for the telephone kiosk at the corner, where I looked through the K's. There was an Oliver Keene living on Danson Street, and I copied down the address. After that I went to the post office and Xeroxed two copies of Hannah's note, and carried them to the park where I sat down on a bench. I'd brought scissors with me; I took one of the Xerox copies and cut out parts of two sentences: *I was so tired and hungry but this morning I know* . . . and then, *should anyone ever find this my name is Hannah.* . . . After doing this I walked back to Fleet Street. It was just nine o'clock, and there were no customers waiting for the shop to open. I hung a BACK AT NOON sign on the door and walked south to find 901 Fleet Street, the address I'd looked up in the yellow pages the night before. I would never have thought of consulting a graphologist if I hadn't passed the sign innumerable times on my way to Amman

Singh's. I'd noticed it months before, and out of curiosity I'd looked up the word in the dictionary, just to be sure: the study of handwriting, it said, for the purpose of character analysis. In the yellow pages the man sounded professional: Joseph Osbourne, followed by the word ACCREDITED, whatever that meant—or by whom—and CONSULTANT. I was hoping he could tell me something about the person who'd written the note.

A distance of six blocks in a city can make as much difference as Dante walking in or out of his Inferno. My block on Fleet Street was a bazaar full of second-hand this and thats, uncertain whether collapse or renewal lay ahead for it, surprisingly prim in its values, still relatively crime-free but hanging on by the skin of its teeth. On sunny days the block looked picturesque, on rainy days forlorn; it trod a very narrow line.

The 900-block had an uncanny resemblance to the 600-block except that it had been shored up, laundered, dipped in paint until it sparkled, and I could guess that its rents were triple that of mine. It even had a few trees, not very old yet, planted among the cobbles. Joseph P. Osbourne, Graphologist, was on the second floor of 901, over a doctor's office that occupied the first floor. I walked up steps that grew progressively shabbier and dustier until by the time I reached the second floor I felt quite at home. On the landing I was met by three doors, all wide open: one to a lavatory, another to an office with desk and chairs, the third a sunny back room that to my practiced eye was obviously J. Osbourne's living quarters. Since the office was empty, I knocked on the open door in the middle and peered inside.

A muffled voice said, "Who is it?"

The voice seemed to come from a sort of tent occupying the middle of the room; at least I couldn't think what else it could be since it was about five feet high,

28

came to a point like a teepee, and had a sheet loosely thrown over it. It was at this moment that I felt a prescient stab of terror at what I was getting into. It simply hadn't occurred to me, it really hadn't, that this quixotic search of mine was going to mean knocking on strange doors and meeting *people,* in this case someone under a sheet. I remembered Dr. Merivale's speeches on Affecting My Environment, and Amman Singh's gentle fables about Letting Go, and their words felt like balloon captions over my head that came together and exploded. I wondered if the man under the tent had heard the explosion. I stopped trembling and said crisply, "Amelia Jones, needing information, please."

The sheet stirred, one corner was lifted, and J. Osbourne crawled out and stood up. "It's early," he said accusingly. "You shouldn't just walk in."

"I knocked," I reminded him.

He wasn't much older than I was, and I wasn't sure he was J. Osbourne. He was wearing blue jeans and no shoes and a wrinkled denim shirt. He had a nice open boyish face, with the skin very taut over its bones, which were arranged into interesting angles. He had dark hair and blue eyes and a thin, intense look about him. He stood there running one hand through his hair and frowning at me. "I work by appointment," he said, "and you've no appointment."

"You're Mr. Osbourne then? I thought you'd be older."

"I *am* older sometimes," he said.

I didn't find that surprising; it seemed a very sensible remark to make. I said, being curious, "Do you sleep under a tent?"

"It's not a tent, it's a pyramid. I was sitting under it meditating." He grasped the tent's apex with one hand and lifted it; it collapsed into vertical rods which he leaned against the wall, sheet and all. "It's a port able one, made to an exact scale of the Cheops one in Egypt."

"Oh," I said.

"You've heard about pyramid power, of course?"

"Of course," I lied. "It just looked like a tent from where I'm standing."

"Well, you might as well stop standing," he said grudgingly, "and explain your popping in like this. I hope you don't mind if I scramble an egg, I've not had breakfast yet."

"Of course not," I said. "I wouldn't have come if it weren't an emergency."

He moved to the stove, cracked an egg into a frying pan, stirred it with a fork and turned on the heat under it. I looked around me. With the tent—the pyramid, that is—removed, it was possible to see the room itself, and I liked it. There was a wicker rocking chair painted canary yellow and upholstered in blue oilcloth. There was a mahogany church pew with a denim cushion, and a desk made out of file cabinets and plywood. One wall was covered with oil paintings, framed sketches, maps, and books. It was a bright, cheerful room, just disorderly enough to prevent pangs of inadequacy in me.

"Okay, show me what you've got," he said, carrying his plate of scrambled egg to the desk and sitting down.

I brought out my envelope, shook the pieces of cut paper out of it, and arranged them in front of him. He looked at them over his egg and then he turned and looked at me. "Photostats!" he said scornfully. "Bits and pieces . . . what kind of job do you think I can do with that?"

"It's handwriting," I protested.

"If you want your money's worth—I charge fifteen dollars—I'll need the original."

I said coldly, "I'd rather not show the original."

30

The telephone on the desk rang. He gave me a curious look as he reached for it and answered. He listened a minute, his face thoughtful. "No, I'd disagree with that, I think the child needs professional help. Right. Juvenile Court at 2 P.M., I'll be there."

He hung up and, seeing the look on my face, he smiled. "I hope you don't assume handwriting analysis is fortunetelling," he said. "I have a degree in psychology and I work with the courts and with the schools, Miss—Miss—"

"Jones. Amelia Jones. If I thought it was fortunetelling I wouldn't be here."

"Good." He turned in his chair and gave me his full attention, his egg only half-eaten. "I don't know why you don't want me to see the original, Amelia, but I have to have more lines for evaluating, I really do." He must have seen the stubbornness in my face because he added patiently, "I need a look at connective forms to see whether they're garlands or arcade, angled or filiforms. I have to look for the constellations or clusters of traits, and laterals. The dotting of i's and crossing of t's is terribly important, and so are the marginal patterns, and then there are the zones—bizonal, trizonal, unizonal. There's the slant of the writing, and fluctuations that might suggest ambivalence, the pressure of the pen on paper, the strokes—ascending, descending or lateral, and whether they're broken or interrupted or fractured. Then there are counterstrokes and endstrokes—protective or directive—and interspaces..."

"Oh," I said, blinking.

"... and with what you've given me—only two lines, I see—I can't do a decent job."

I sighed and reluctantly groped in my shoulder bag, brought out the original letter and gave it to him.

"Thanks," he said and bent over it. "Written under

31

some pressure," he murmured, pointing vaguely at the middle of the paper. "Interesting handwriting."

"Man or woman?" I asked.

But he had begun to read the letter now, I could see that. I dropped my eyes and stared intently at his egg, which lay on his plate cooling and congealing. After a moment he said in an astonished voice, "Where on earth did you get this? Who wrote it?"

"I found it," I said, my eyes remaining fixed on his egg. "I don't know who wrote it."

"But shouldn't you take this to the police?"

I hated explaining. When you're not too strong a person, people can take things away from you so easily. I said, "I happen to own the Ebbtide Shop at 688 Fleet Street, and when I bought the shop there was an old hurdy-gurdy included. Last night I was playing the hurdy-gurdy and it got stuck, and I found the note inside. That's two months it's been there. At eight this morning I visited the former owner and he looked up his records and found that he'd bought the hurdy-gurdy six months ago. That's a long time. I don't see what the police could do, do you?"

"No," he said, sounding stunned. "But then what do you have in mind?"

I wrested my gaze from his egg and found him looking baffled but kind. I said, "From Mr. Georgerakis I have the name of the man who sold it to him. If I go and see him he may know who Hannah is. Or was. Or he may give me another name."

"You believe the note is authentic?"

I nodded. "It feels authentic. I'm hoping you'll tell me more about the person who wrote it."

"Even if they're dead?"

"Even if they're dead."

He looked at me for a long time. He seemed to be having trouble remaining professional. "Right," he

32

said. "None of my business, either, is it. Except—" He turned on me angrily. "But if the note should be real, the operative word here is murder, have you thought about that?"

I flushed. "I can't really explain, it's just something I feel I have to look into. Wouldn't you?"

"I don't know," he said, looking young again and unprofessional. "Amelia, is it? Amelia, will you for heaven's sake—" He stopped. "Damn it, my egg's cold."

I giggled. "I know."

"Coffee?"

"All right."

I sat and drank coffee while he studied the letter and made a great many notes on a sheet of paper next to it. I learned that graphology couldn't determine the sex of a person but only their masculine and feminine qualities. Hannah appeared to have a fairly equal proportion of each, with perhaps the feminine a shade more persistent. I learned that Hannah was somewhat introverted, and definitely a reclusive type. Her writing—until she was proven to be otherwise I had to consider her a woman—was sensitive and artistic. She was basically a generous person, and reliable. There was some sexual repression but nothing abnormal there. She was healthy and educated, had a strong vein of common sense, and along with her flair for the artistic she had considerable executive capabilities.

"No fool, your Hannah," said J. Osbourne, putting down his pen. "I can type up a detailed analysis for you tonight, giving you the full picture, but I'd say she's a perfectly sane person—assuming she's female—who ran her life well, would be generous with those closest to her but not overly outgoing with people in general, preferring a quiet orderly life. She'd insist on privacy—it would mean a great deal to her, perhaps be something of a fetish with her. But except for these tenden-

33

cies toward withdrawal, and a preference for control over spontaneity, this is a balanced, reliable, fairly realistic person, with no signs of abnormality, psychosis, disease, or hysteria. This note was written under pressure but the pressure is muted at the beginning. Actually the first few lines are more reflective than agitated. As the note progresses you can see by the pressure of the pen on the paper that there's a growing anger, a growing haste, a sense of being—well, pressured."

"Or frightened," I said quietly. "You make her sound—nice."

He nodded. "I think she was. And I wish like hell I could have told you she was unbalanced, sick, or mad, the sort who writes notes and hides them in hurdy-gurdies every day. Then, damn it, you'd go home and forget about her, which I hope you'll do, anyway. If you don't, you've placed me in a lousy position, you know."

"How so?" I asked curiously.

His lips tightened. "I'll have to worry about you."

"Oh, you mustn't," I said earnestly. "It's very nice of you but you mustn't feel that way. An hour ago you didn't even know I existed. It wasn't your fault I brought you a letter like this, although I did try to keep you from seeing it," I pointed out.

"Yes, you did," he agreed dryly. "Where are you off to now?"

"To see Oliver Keene, who used to own the hurdy-gurdy."

"Look, you live with your parents?" he asked.

I shook my head.

"Close friends?"

I shook my head.

"Hell," he said, running a hand through his hair again, "then do me one favor, will you? Call me tonight and tell me you're all right." He rummaged in his desk and produced a card. "This is my number, I'll be here." When I looked surprised he smiled faintly. "Look, it isn't only that, I'm curious, I want to know what you find out, okay? I begin to feel I know Hannah myself."

"All right," I said. "I will." But of course I wouldn't. I counted out fifteen dollars and placed them on his desk.

I'd reached the door when he said, looking after me, "My friends call me Os, by the way. Short for Osbourne."

Struck shy by this I said inanely, "I'm called Amelia," and fearing this sounded flippant I turned scarlet and fled.

3

Danson Street was in the warehouse district over by the river. I caught a bus across town that deposited me in front of a store with a brand-new window and the name S. S. Schwarz, Skull Cap Mfr., overhead. In the window, on shelves, sat tall, conical spools of thread like so many Turkish fezes, and under them a pile of completed yarmulkes. I crossed the street to number 305, where there was also a new window set into a dingy wooden front. A really good painting hung there: palette-knife work, the paint thick and juicy and clotted with dizzying whorls of blue that sucked the eye round and round and down into the vortex where a single eye stared at me unblinkingly. The hand-printed card at its base read COMPULSION by Oliver Keene. I rather liked that. I have my compulsive moments, too: I get sucked into maelstroms of frenetic activity that keep me from sitting down and giving up, which happens when I experience feelings of total inadequacy. I sometimes think if you harnessed enough compulsive people together their tensions could probably supply energy to a fair-sized city.

It was possible, although I didn't care to admit it, that I would presently find myself growing compulsive about this unknown and mysterious Hannah.

I pushed the buzzer and the woman who opened the door at number 305 looked as if she'd never experienced an inadequate moment in her life. She was easily six feet tall, an Amazon of a woman with a face like a Barbie doll. She wore jodhpurs and a white shirt open almost to her navel, and her curves were breakneck; I must have said "wow" without realizing it, or perhaps my eyes did, because she grinned.

"Honey," she said, "it's God-given and there's nothing I can do about it except hold out for a man with a million bucks. What do you want?"

"I'm looking for Oliver Keene." Her grin was as wholesome as cornflakes but it still left me feeling I'd been a fool to stop my chest exercises.

"Ollie? You'd better come in and wait, he's dashed out for some alizarin crimson." She pushed the door wider and I followed her inside. "I'm Daisy," she called over her shoulder.

"I'm Amelia Jones," I answered politely, feeling about ten years old, and 20–18–20 next to those curves.

It was a nice studio. It was the first one I'd ever seen outside of films, and Oliver Keene must have seen the same films I did, because it matched. There was a huge wooden easel under the skylight, a circular model stand nearby, and paintings stashed in cubbyholes and leaning against walls. The room held a pungent odor of turp and paint and mildew that tickled my nostrils. The easel was empty but there were drawings all over the drafting table in the corner, and out of curiosity I walked over and looked at them. Not exactly porno but cheap, I thought, all of them lascivious nudes, and all of them Daisy: wearing only a shawl, riding a bicycle under a floppy hat, or naked in the sand. They probably paid well.

"So what did you want to see him about?" Daisy asked, looking me over. "If you came to ask about modeling, honey, your bones are great but this week he's doing sexy calendars. Twelve undressed girls, all of them me, and I don't think—" She had perched on a tall stool, where she towered over me.

"I appreciate your tact," I told her, smiling—it was impossible not to like her—"but I came to ask about a hurdy-gurdy he sold to the Ebbtide Shop in November. I'm tracing it for a customer."

"Oh," she said, thinking about this and nibbling on her index finger. "Yeah, he told me he sold it, the bastard. It was mine, not his, we had a fight and he sold it."

I brightened. "You mean it was yours?"

She nodded.

"But that's great, I don't have to see him at all, then. Could you tell me where you bought it?"

"I didn't buy it, it was a gift."

"Then who—"

But Daisy was regarding me now with caution. "So if I told you the guy's name what would you do?"

"Pay a call and ask him where *he* bought it."

She shook her head. "No way, kid."

"Why?"

She shook her head again. "No *way*."

"I don't understand," I pleaded. "I'm just tracing it for a customer, it's all perfectly innocent."

"It may be as innocent as a meadow of clover," she said, looking amused, "and I can see innocence is your bag, honey—I'll bet you're still a virgin—but a girl's got to think of her future."

"But this is important—"

"Like I told you—the hurdy-gurdy was a present. Along with a diamond clip and earrings, and a cash award for services rendered."

"Oh," I said, blinking. "I don't have to know that, do I?"

"Don't be dumb," she said. "If I told you the guy's name he'd assume I'd just as easily tell his wife or anybody else who comes asking. A girl's got to think about these things. I'm really fond of Ollie, I live with him, he's a great guy, but Ollie's going to be doing porno calendars twenty years from now and taking empties to the store for pocket money. Sorry, honey. Cheat a little. Make up some names for your silly customer, I've got to protect my friends. You think this is going to last?" she demanded, with a glance downward, at her voluptuous body.

"You'd still be six feet tall," I pointed out dryly. I hated her stubbornness but it equaled mine. I drew the letter out of my shoulder bag and handed it to her. "Before you say no again, at least know what the real story is. I'm not tracing the hurdy-gurdy for a customer, the hurdy-gurdy belongs to me and I found this inside of it last night."

"Holding out on me, kid?" she said good-naturedly, but she was curious enough to take it. She moved closer to the light and read it, and then she read it again. "What is this, anyway? Who's this Hannah?"

"That's what I want to find out," I told her. "Does

39

your friend—has he mentioned anyone named Hannah?"

She frowned. "His wife's name is Sylvia, I know that. God how I know it. Sylvia doesn't understand him, Sylvia's frigid, Sylvia's this and Sylvia's that." But she was interested, I could see that. "Look, whoever this is, she has to be dead now."

"Not just dead," I pointed out. "Murdered."

She was nibbling on her finger again, her eyes on the note. "Which makes you some kind of a nut, doesn't it?" But she said it idly, without force.

"Someone locked her up in her own house," I said, watching her. "They didn't give her food or let her sleep until she signed something. She was a woman and you're a woman."

She shrugged. "There's a lot of stuff like that going on now," she said vaguely.

"This had to be for money."

"Lucky Hannah, to have some."

"They got away with it."

"I'd sure be interested in what you figure *you* could do about it," she said.

The door opened and closed behind us sharply, and abruptly the atmosphere changed. It had been good until then, the two of us drawn together over the note, a fleeting intimacy between us as we thought about Hannah, but now I felt Daisy's withdrawal. She said, not looking up, "Hi, Ollie."

I turned to look at Oliver Keene. He was big and good-looking, and as dramatic as Daisy in his own way: they matched. But a grain of coarseness had settled over him like silt, a coarseness that my Amazon friend could easily acquire, too, in a few years. His hair was thick and wavy, a brassy blond color, and his eyes a startling blue in a leathery tanned face. He looked about forty or forty-five. He wore a windbreaker over dirty corduroys, and when he smiled there was a gap in his teeth on one side. Although his smile was warm and hearty I thought he looked tired, as if he knew that his girl slept around and nobody was ever going to buy the painting in the window. "So hello," he said. "Company, I see."

"Not really," Daisy said, nibbling her finger. "She got lost, she was asking directions so I brought her in. She's just going now, aren't you, kid?"

"Reluctantly," I said, giving her an unforgiving glance.

"You can't win 'em all," she said with a shrug, deliberately looking me in the eye. "Nice meeting you, kid," she said. "So long."

I put the letter back in my shoulder bag and there were tears of frustration in my eyes. I walked out with the taste of rejection in my mouth, and I've never handled rejection well. I crossed the street to the bus stop, trying not to think what this meant, trying to postpone the failure of it until I got home and could really cry. Through my tears I saw the door to the studio open across the street and a blurred Daisy appear. She waved and called, "Hey, kid!"

She crossed the street calmly, not hurrying at all, until she reached my side and looked down at me. "Of course you're a kook, you know that," she said.

"Maybe," I said.

"Okay, kid, I'll throw in the towel, but on conditions. Conditions, you understand? I hope you've got paper with you."

I dug out my notebook, my hands trembling.

"The conditions are as follows," she said. "You tell him Miss Doris Tucci sent you. We keep it formal, very formal. And I *bought* the hurdy-gurdy from him, you hear? I don't even know the man, I don't know him from a hole in the wall. Promise?"

41

"Promise," I said, smiling at her through my tears. "What changed your mind?"

A truck passed, and the driver nearly fell out of his front seat staring at her but she'd probably stopped noticing this sort of thing. When she'd written the name and address in my notebook she looked down at me and grinned. "What the hell," she said humorously, "I figure if I'm ever in the same situation—locked up by a guy but *not* for my jewels, honey—it's nice to know I can call on you. And let me know sometime what you dig up."

"I will," I said, "and thank you."

She walked across the street and then she turned and called after me crossly, "And try brushing your hair a hundred strokes a day; it doesn't *have* to look like that, kid."

It was half-past twelve when I got back to the shop and opened it up again, and by that time some of my triumph and excitement had worn off. The address Daisy had given me was a New York City Park Avenue address, which meant I was going to have to venture still further out of my cocoon and leave both the shop and my city behind me. This turned my victory with Daisy a little sour. I have my own safety zones like everyone else and I found this unsettling, not having visited New York City since I was a child. At the moment it might as well have been Vladivostok or Vera Cruz. I think it was at this point—entering my familiar shop and realizing that the next stop was New York— that I came closest to giving up the idea and accepting the fact that I lacked the iron nerve and stamina for tilting at windmills.

However, a decorator from uptown walked in soon after that, a nice ginger-haired little man who spent more than an hour poking around the shop. When he left he'd bought two of the merry-go-round horses and a bolt of pre-war emerald-green velvet that I didn't even know I had. He said he'd be back with a repair man to look at the jukebox, and he left me his card: ENOCH INTERIORS. A link with a decorator was a pretty dazzling prospect. It also reminded me that I would soon be cleaned out of all the good stuff, leaving me with the thirty-two gaudy plates hand-stamped SOUVENIR OF TRAFTON, all those dented coffee pots and cartons of rejected wigs, the cases of violet-colored plastic flowers, and of course those hideous bathrobes of Mr. Georgerakis'. Obviously I would have to pry myself loose soon, anyway, and begin going to auctions; this placed the trip to New York on a practical basis that reduced my anxiety over it. In fact I was feeling confident again, and really quite sanguine about it all, when J. Osbourne, Graphologist, strolled into my shop just before five o'clock.

"Hello," he said, looking very neat and professional in a shirt and tie. "I still owe you that written report, it's part of the deal, so I brought it over personally."

"Thanks," I said, taking the two neatly typed sheets of paper and placing them on the cash register.

"I thought I'd find out what progress you made this morning, too."

It suddenly felt like quite a bit of progress. "I have another lead," I told him. "I have a new name."

"You're awfully determined. You know," he said, frowning, "you look about sixteen years old but you can't be."

"I'm twenty-two."

He nodded. "I'm thirty-one. If you weren't so thin," he added sternly, "you'd look older. Do you eat enough?"

"Of course I eat enough," I told him. "I eat like a horse. I don't see what that has to do with anything."

"I was leading up to inviting you to go out with me

43

to dinner," he said. "I was hoping you could go. I can offer Italian or Chinese."

I felt a stab of panic. It was happening at last and I wasn't ready for it, I hadn't even had time to brush my hair one hundred strokes. I'd been planning to walk over to see Amman Singh and tell him about Hannah, but here was someone who already knew about Hannah. I looked at Joe Osbourne and he looked at me, waiting. I felt as if I were poised on the edge of a waterfall and looking over the edge. I heard myself say, truthfully enough, "I'd love to," and making this jump I wondered if I was going to land on jagged rocks, in a quiet pond or be swept away in the rapids.

The Chinese restaurant was full of squat, smiling little Buddhas tucked in niches, and the booths were wicker, painted Chinese red. It was very colorful, and of course it was located in his block, not mine. After he'd ordered War Tip Har, which Joe said was highly recommendable, he asked me about Daisy and I told him all about my morning.

"I can see this is very educational for you," he said, looking amused. "Daisy sounds like quite a girl."

I conceded cautiously that it could be, and that she was.

"Have you always lived in Trafton?" he asked.

"Yes, but on Walnut Street, out by the park."

"And your parents?"

"My father died four years ago, my mother when I was eleven."

He winced. "I'm sorry. That must have been rough."

"It was, a little." A small shrug. Very casual voice. Bright smile. I *know* I'm not the only person in the world to whom this has happened, I know there are people being tortured in political prisons and girls my age dying somewhere of starvation, I *know* this, but it

44

sits there, a bone in my throat, an undigested pain; it happened to me, after all. "And your family?" I asked.

He seemed to have a family right out of a television sitcom: humorous lawyer father, understanding mother, two mischievous sisters.... That's what made him so nice, I suppose, and I was realizing even before dessert how very nice he was. He called himself a casualty of the sixties—he'd personally met Dr. Martin Luther King, Jr., he knew all the verses of "We Shall Overcome," and had been in peace vigils and protests and marches—but, so far as I could see, the only casualty this had produced was the law career he'd planned. He had intended to be a lawyer like his father but instead he'd veered into psychology.

I was fascinated by this glimpse into another life. "And then what?"

"Then two years of graduate school, after which I went to Switzerland to study graphology. The Institute for Applied Psychology in Zurich. They've trained quite a few graphologists."

Switzerland, no less. A real sophisticate. And here I was, edgy about a trip to New York less than a hundred miles away.

Over dessert—spumoni—he asked if I was going to look up Daisy's diamond-earring boy friend.

"Oh yes," I said. "His name—well, I'd better not tell you that, had I—but he lives on Park Avenue, which you have to admit is a nicer neighborhood than Danson Street. I'll try to pick up a few things for the shop, too."

"So when will you go?"

I'd had time to think about this. "Probably Sunday," I told him, "and come back late Monday. That way I can straddle both the weekend and a weekday. I mean, it's all rather obscure, finding him at home, but this way there'll be two possibilities. I don't want to call him first; he might refuse to see me."

45

"Especially when he remembers to whom he gave the hurdy-gurdy."

"Yes." I was realizing, thinking about auctions, that eventually I was going to have to buy a car to carry things, so we spent the rest of dinner talking about cars, and which had better mileage, because I am very energy-oriented. I think ecology is terribly important because this planet is getting so soiled, and you can't just use a vacuum cleaner on it.

"Do you know how to drive?"

"Oh yes, that was one of Dr. Merivale's projects."

"Dr. Merivale?"

And so we came to Dr. Merivale, and I managed to keep that very light, but I could see the puzzled look in his eyes. I did hope he wasn't going to be one of *those* people, but I thought I might as well find out early, and so I asked him. "Does it shock you about the psychiatry?"

"God no," he said. "It's just that you seem—I'm glad you've stopped seeing him because I'd hate to see you lose the kind of quirky quality you have. I like it."

"Quirky?"

He grinned. "You keep me guessing. When I asked you to dinner you looked terrified. When I met you this morning on your mission—I daresay having a mission helps, doesn't it?—you were so confident. You strike me as very honest and direct and warm, a bit of a nut basically—different—but then you bolt. I see it happen: advance and retreat."

"I'm very insecure," I told him.

"I think that somewhere inside of you," he said solemnly, "there is a very fat Amelia struggling to get out."

I laughed. He paid the bill and we walked slowly back to my shop. I unlocked the door and we went upstairs to my apartment where I showed him the hurdy-gurdy and he played it a few times. He liked the merry-go-round horse, too. We listened to a few records, not talking much, and then he said he had to type a few reports before morning, because schools were closing and it was his last busy week before the summer's lull. When he said good night he did a curious thing; he reached out and touched my hair, experimentally, sort of, and then he kissed me lightly on the cheek and left.

4

Three days later, on Sunday afternoon, I walked under the canopy of the Heathcliffe Arms on Park Avenue, smiled pleasantly at the doorman and rang the buzzer of apartment 1023, Colonel Morgan Alcourt. I was wearing my high suede boots—rather hot for a May day—and a beige corduroy skirt and jacket. I was frankly trembling in those boots, but I think there must be a little of the actress in everyone, or else when one is terrified the adrenal juices start flowing like mad. A voice rasped in my ear, "Yes, who is it?" and I said over the intercom, "Amelia Jones about a hurdy-gurdy."

"Jones? Hurdy-gurdy?"

"Jones, hurdy-gurdy." I kept it terse, thinking this might be mystifying enough to get me through the door; if I was asked to elaborate I knew I'd be sunk.

"Get Alphonse," barked the voice. "Doorman."

I fetched the doorman and he took over. "A young woman, sir, looks very pleasant," he said, looking me over objectively. "What? Oh no, Colonel, wearing a proper little suit"—he winked at me—"and those high boots the ladies wear now. Something about one of those musical instruments you collect."

So the colonel *collected* hurdy-gurdies; no wonder the word hadn't thrown him. "Yes, sir, I'll send her up," he said, and he winked at me again. "The colonel's very fussy."

"Well," I said earnestly, wondering what the doorman had thought of Daisy, "you can't be too careful these days." On this note I strolled inside, and the elevator soon lifted me silently toward the penthouse.

When the doors of the elevator slid open I stepped out into a lobby—he had a whole lobby to himself—and a man in a white jacket was waiting for me. *Not* the colonel: this chap was Asian and looked very remote, very shuttered, as if he'd wiped away every hint of personality along with the lint on the glassware. "This way, miss," he said; he turned and led me over thick carpeting through a short hallway and into a huge, uncluttered room with a breathtaking view of the city.

And there was the colonel.

He wasn't at all what I'd imagined. He stood about five feet four inches high and the huge room made him look even smaller, a little lost, even pathetic. He stood very erect, but aside from his posture there was nothing at all commanding about him. As I walked toward him I thought he must be shy because he looked at me and then away, then back, then away again and down, as if

49

I'd brought too much light in with me and it blinded him. But when I drew closer I realized that it wasn't shyness: there was something terribly naked about his eyes, a hurt, pleading look, a begging. If anyone ought to be wearing dark glasses, I thought, it should be the colonel, and suddenly I found it as painful to look at him as he did me.

"But I don't know you," he said in surprise, sounding aggrieved. His voice was well modulated but there was a hint of petulance in it. I was terribly glad he had money, because in some unaccountable way he looked completely defenseless. Or perhaps when you have a great deal of money you don't accumulate defenses.

"No," I said in my best, most reassuring and ladylike voice, "and I'm ever so grateful to you for seeing me, I'm from the Ebbtide Curio and Antique Shop in Trafton. Amelia Jones." I put out my hand, which he reluctantly accepted, and it was like grasping a damp towel.

"Mmmm . . . I see," he murmured, dropping my hand.

"I'm tracing a hurdy-gurdy," I told him, very businesslike and trying to ignore the fact that his eyes had dropped now to my bosom, which he was regarding speculatively. When his eyes remained fixed on my bosom and then ran down to my hips I decided not to be so reassuring. "A Miss Doris Tucci gave me your name."

That brought his eyes up in a hurry. He looked astonished, frightened, and then angry, and suddenly he didn't seem pathetic any more: the anger was quick and nasty. I said hastily, "A Mr. Georgerakis owned the hurdy-gurdy and bought it from a Mr. Oliver Keene, who bought it from Miss Tucci, and Miss Tucci has said she purchased it"—I lingered over that word— "from you sometime within the year. Although she

50

couldn't recall just how, or where, she did recall your name."

I felt I'd now preserved Daisy's future for her, although my blood ran cold at the thought of her with this man, and I added, "I'm tracing the hurdy-gurdy, it's terribly important."

"Miss Tucci," he repeated, blinking.

"I have a snapshot of the hurdy-gurdy," I said. I'd bought a Polaroid for the occasion and had shot it from several angles; I brought the photo from my shoulder bag.

"Ah yes ... mmmmm," he murmured, staring at it. "Miss Tucci. Yes, I do believe ... I think I met her at a cocktail party, yes." The anger had been extinguished and he darted a sly, sideways glance at me, perhaps to see if there was irony in my gaze. "But really, you know, this instrument is of very little value except as a conversation piece, I don't understand your interest. You say you're tracing it?"

I was ready for him. I said crisply, "Yes, it's become both an insurance and a police matter. I really can't be more specific except that it's important—very important—to us to find its original owner in the United States."

"Mmmmm ... I see, yes," he said, blinking. "Well, I'm afraid I can't tell you who the original owner was. For myself, I bought it from Robert Lamandale here in New York. The actor, you know."

I didn't know, but I was glad he remembered. I whipped out my notebook. "Could you repeat that name, please?"

"Lamandale," he said, and spelled it out for me. "Don't know where he's living now but he's in town somewhere. Very fine old family. Acts in plays."

Having watched me write down the name he sud-

51

denly relaxed and turned arch. "But I must clear up one detail, my dear young lady," he said, giving me a glance that could only be described as coy. "That," he said, pointing at the snapshot, "is not a hurdy-gurdy."

"Oh?"

"Come, I must educate you," he said, and grasped my arm. He must have decided that if I was unexpected I was at least harmless and could provide him with an audience, although his arm pulled me closer to him than I appreciated. I fell into step with him, and walking practically thigh to thigh we passed through a pair of mahogany doors and into a room that looked like something borrowed from the Metropolitan Museum. Skylights bathed the walls with a luminous, clear pale light, glass-covered exhibits marched down the center of the room, and the walls were hung with all kinds of exotic objects.

"Now here are your *real* hurdy-gurdies," he said, mercifully releasing me. "What *you* are tracing, my dear, is a hand organ, a mere street instrument, and a complete corruption of the true hurdy-gurdy. *Quite* different."

His lips curled contemptuously, showing small rabbit-like teeth. Obviously he was a purist but I could see his point: there *was* a difference. The instruments he was pointing out looked like bulky, foreshortened violins or lutes, and aside from the fact that they appeared to have handles at one end there was no resemblance at all to my hurdy-gurdy. Or hand organ.

"An incredibly old instrument, the hurdy-gurdy," he said, very much the authority now, "but for most of its life it was called an organistrum. It's history is so long that I can tell you that Odo of Cluny wrote a treatise on the organistrum in the ninth century. It wasn't called a hurdy-gurdy until the eighteenth century."

"I see," I murmured, trying to strike the right note of interest.

"Take a look at this one," he said, pointing.

"Good heavens, it's long!"

"Isn't it?" he said, beaming at me. "It measures five feet in length. Thirteenth century. Two people had to work it, they sat in chairs with the instrument across their laps and one worked the wheel, the other the key rods and tangents.

"But you can see the growing sophistication as time went on," he added, darting from one glass cage to another and beckoning me to follow him. "That thirteenth-century hurdy-gurdy had only three strings. By the sixteenth century—see this one?—there were four strings, and over here you see a seventeenth-century organistrum with five strings. In the eighteenth century the instruments were considerably refined. They were given six strings with a melody compass of two octaves."

"Amazing," I said, feeling that I was learning somewhat more about hurdy-gurdies than I needed to know. "What's that beauty over there?"

"A *vielle à roue*—rebuilt lute," he said eagerly. "The one next to it's a *vielle organisée*, with a miniature organ in the body. That's eighteenth century."

"Really lovely," I said, and they were. They were made of fantastic woods, and carved beautifully by hand. Some had ivory inlays and others were brightly painted. He opened up the cage and brought one out for me to hold.

"My collection," he said, watching me, "is considered finer than the one at the Victoria and Albert Museum in England."

"But when did they turn into hand organs?" I asked.

"Well," he said forgivingly, "they enjoyed a very real

upsurge of popularity in France in the eighteenth century until the French revolution came along. That's when they were called hurdy-gurdies. They were probably corrupted in the next century—the nineteenth—by the Italian street boy who strolled through town with it and in due course discarded it for a form of organ to which he could add a strap and a stick for mobility."

"I see."

We had reached the end of the room and were face to face with some rather appalling objects hung on the wall. He gave me a sly glance and said, "Interested in torture, Miss Jones?"

Startled, I said, "Not particularly, no."

"Not even—whips?" he suggested playfully.

"Definitely not," I said firmly.

"Over the years," he confided with considerable relish, "I have collected a very remarkable group of torture instruments and I believe you'd find them quite fascinating, Miss Jones. Would you care to join me in a drink?"

I wondered what Amman Singh would say about this little man. "Thank you, no," I told him, "I really have to go."

"I don't often have the opportunity to meet such a sweet young lady," he said archly, and emphasized this by taking a step closer to me.

I fought the urge to move a step back. I said in a clear firm voice, "No—I really have to leave now."

"There is, for instance, one particular instrument that is inserted up—"

I gasped, "Going now—friend downstairs waiting—thanks so much," which mercifully blocked out the rest of his sentence. Leaving him there in the middle of the room I raced back through his living room, down the short hall to the lobby, punched the down button, and didn't feel safe until I was in the lobby again. Nasty little sado-masochist, I thought.

"Get what you wanted?" called Alphonse the doorman cheerfully.

I felt like saying, "I did and he didn't" but I only smiled and headed for a telephone directory to look up Robert Lamandale, and then I flagged down a taxi.

But I was thinking about the colonel and wondering what might have bent him out of shape like that, because he wouldn't have been born that way. I always think it's a matter of a person coming up against an immovable object somewhere along the way, like a foot trying to grow normally but meeting the solid wall of a shoe, the bones and flesh pressing and pressing without finding any space to expand, until the bones have to bend and twist into deformity. It had to be an absence of love, of course, it nearly always is, which is a subject on which I can expound at great length, being experienced. For instance, there was a time when I used to read all the books about love being published; I felt if I read enough of them I might find the one particular book that would tell me how to be lovable. I was that naïve, along with all the other people who kept those books on the best-seller list. I remember scanning one of these in a book store a couple of years ago. It was a very hot day, and my feet hurt, and I was feeling very lonely, and this book said that no one should end a day without touching someone, and also without telling another person they loved them. The whole book was about this, and at first I stood there feeling rage boil up inside of me because I mean, how many of us *know* anybody to touch or to say "I love you" to? But at the time I believed this writer, so I went home and selected a few names from the telephone book, I called them and I said, "I love you."

It didn't do a thing for me, of course. One woman

threatened to call the police, and a man asked if I was some kind of pervert or something. It would have been nice, I thought, if someone could have said, "I don't know who you are but I love you, too." But then I was always writing scenarios that never happened.

Robert Lamandale lived on East Ninth Street, and such was my naïveté that I believed anything *east* in New York was much finer than west; the colonel's remark about Lamandale coming from an old family had substantiated this, and so as the cab drove through and down streets I kept waiting for an elegant neighborhood to materialize. It didn't. I found myself growing increasingly nervous the farther we went and the cab driver, catching my eye in the mirror, must have seen my nervousness, too. "You sure you got the address right, miss?" he asked.

I read it to him and he nodded. "That's it okay. Just down this block."

We drew up in front of eight garbage pails piled along the sidewalk, with litter spilling over to the ground. Number 218 was a tall brick building surrounded by rubble; the whole block looked like something out of a war movie, with holes gaping like extracted teeth. The door of number 218 was half open, with two panes of glass smashed out of it. I said, "Do you think you could wait for me? I don't expect to be long, he may not even be at home."

"How long?"

"Ten minutes?"

"Okay. You look like a nice girl, I won't even ask for a deposit."

"You can hold my raincoat," I told him gravely. "It's the only one I've got."

It felt like leaving another safety zone as I scurried up the half-rotted stairs and pressed the buzzer under Lamandale, apartment 12. Nothing happened and I began pressing all the buzzers until someone finally buzzed me in. I started up the stairs and had reached the second landing when I heard steps racing down toward me. I stopped and waited. A man came into view, taking the steps two at a time, and as he sped past me I said, "Could you tell me where I'll find apartment 12?"

"Twelve! Who are you looking for?"

"Robert Lamandale."

He stopped just two steps below me and looked at me. When I'd first glimpsed him crashing down the stairs toward me I'd thought he was about thirty years old but now I saw that he was closer to forty, or perhaps even forty-five. He was small and slender and very compact, with a friendly, cheerful face, an upturned nose and thin, merry lips. But he dyed his hair too dark a shade of brown and there were hammocks of flesh under his eyes, and small lines etched around his mouth.

"Look, dear," he said, "I'm Robert Lamandale but I've got a call from my agent. I can't stop. What is it you want?"

"It's about a hurdy-gurdy you owned once and sold. I'm trying to trace it."

"Hurdy-gurdy? Hurdy-gurdy? Is that all?"

"It's terribly important."

"So is my audition, darling, there aren't that many calls for aging ingenues. Did I ever have a hurdy-gurdy?"

I handed him the snapshot and he laughed.

"Oh God, yes . . . *that*. Certainly brings back happier days. I bought it at auction in Maine, back when I had money."

"But do you remember the name of the auction house, or where it came from?"

"Oh yes. A relative of mine—a cousin, actually—

57

sold off her entire estate at auction. I bought the hurdy-gurdy as a souvenir, a memento. Purest indulgence."

"Yes, but what's her name?"

He was already six steps below me now. "Leonora Harrington," he called over his shoulder.

"How can I find her?" I called after him. "Is she still alive?"

"Only semi and quasi, the poor soul," he said, turning at the next landing to look up at me. "In a private hospital near Portland, Maine, somewhere. Psychiatric hospital. Nice meeting you," he added cheerfully, and he was gone.

I hurried down to the next landing and shouted after him, "But can't you remember the name of the hospital?"

"Sorry," he shouted back, and I heard the front door slam below me.

I stood there in a shaft of sunlight watching the dust motes lazily rise and fall, and then I heard the door open and he shouted up the stairwell, "Try Greenwood Hospital. Green *something*, anyway."

I called out, "Thanks!" and then I raced down after him, thinking to offer him a lift uptown in my waiting taxi, but when I arrived on the street he had already wheeled out a small motorbike from a locked shed attached to the building. "Thanks," I shouted again. "I mean *really* thanks."

He grinned. "No charge," he called, and with a flip of his hand he buzzed off.

I climbed back into my taxi and gave the driver the name of my hotel. I hoped Robert Lamandale got the job; I really liked him.

5

I returned to Trafton on Monday night with, among
other things, a first edition of Gruble's *The Maze in the
Heart of the Castle*. I could see that at this rate I was
rapidly losing ground; I'd paid sixty-five dollars for the
first edition, and counted it a bargain at that, but I
certainly wasn't going to show any profit buying out-
of-print first editions of a book I already owned and
had read as a child until its pages were tattered. I knew
I'd never want to sell it. I consoled myself by remembering that a box of Bavarian cuckoo clocks was on its
way by truck, as well as a crate of blue willow ware,
and that I'd bid next to nothing on a trunk of Indian
fabrics that just missed being garish and would make

awfully good saris, or bedspreads, skirts, or curtains. I had also experienced my first auction.

It was past ten o'clock when I climbed the stairs to my two rooms over the shop. The refrigerator had gone wild again and I gave it a kick to quiet it; it settled gratefully into a sonorous purr. I opened a can of chowder, made a pot of coffee, buttered two slices of bread and sat down at the battered kitchen table to thumb through the pages of the book I'd so recklessly bought. I was really glad now that I'd bought it; it took away the lingering taste of Colonel Morgan Alcourt completely. Here were the same beloved illustrations by Howard Pyle of Colin meeting the Grand Odlum, of Colin fighting alone against the Wos, and of the Conjurer building a rainbow for Colin. When I was eleven years old nobody had ever told me about *Winnie the Pooh* or *The Wind in the Willows* or the Hobbits: *this* was my book.

My favorite part had always been Colin's meeting with the Despas. When he began his search the Grand Odlum had told him, "If search you must, then I can only give you this advice: the important thing is to carry the sun with you, inside of you at every moment, against the darkness. Because there will be a great and terrifying darkness."

The Despas were the darkest, which is why I loved best of all Colin's outwitting them. When he reached them he was exhausted and ill from his journey and the Despas sheltered him in their dark caves out of the wind. They gave him food and safety and chided him for his precociousness. They told him that beyond their valley lay high cliffs and an intolerable cold, that he was naïve and a fool to think of going on, that he really must give up. Colin listened and believed, finding their dark caves womblike and hypnotic, until one day he remembered the Grand Odlum's words and he realized

60

the Despas had nearly extinguished the sun in his heart because they had none at all in their own.

But when he told the Despas that it was time for him to leave they said that he was theirs now forever, and they would never let him go.

I turned the pages until I found the illustration I loved most, and I was smiling now. Eleven years later, and grown up, so to speak, I had to concede that the drawing still brought a quickening of my heart: that moment when Colin, trapped and desperate, tears away the animal skins the Despas have hung over every entrance and opening of the cave, and then races to the solitary lantern and lights torch after torch until the Despas are blinded by light, and he escapes them.

It wasn't until I was twelve that I realized the book was a miniature *Pilgrim's Progress,* and it wasn't until I met Dr. Merivale that I understood why the Despas had affected me so: I'd been born among them, I'd lived with one for half of my life.

Carefully, very carefully, I rewrapped the book and put it away in the drawer with my bankbooks, and then I returned to the pile of brochures I'd collected on cars and vans because I'd decided I was going to drive to Portland. I also realized I was growing very interested in life, as if it suddenly had a great deal to offer, but somehow, because of this, I didn't want to call Joe and tell him I was back. I was beginning to feel extremely vulnerable where Joe was concerned. I didn't want to expect anything from him, which of course meant that already I was expecting too much: I was looking forward to seeing him again and terrified that I might not. It is very uphill work being insecure, and profoundly exhausting.

I didn't hear from Joe the next morning, and so, during my lunch hour I doggedly went out and looked at cars by myself. This whittled down my defenses enough to telephone him from a pay station.

"I thought you'd never call," he said. "How long are you going to play games?"

I said weakly that I didn't know what he meant.

"Of course you do. You got back last night, didn't you?"

"Yes, but it was late and I thought—"

"You thought I'd say Amelia Who."

I decided to ignore this. I said there was a car, a small truck and a van, and I hoped he knew something that might help.

"I'll be over at five but how was New York, what did you find out? Any luck?"

"I saw two people, a hurdy-gurdy collector and an actor," I told him, "and next I have to go to Maine."

"My God it's like a scavenger hunt," he said. "See you at five."

It was a busy afternoon. Enoch Interiors arrived with a mechanic and they poked and prodded the insides of the old nineteen-forties jukebox. "It's so deliciously camp," gloated Mr. Enoch, rubbing his hands together. The bell over the shop door jangled frequently: one of Mr. Georgerakis' weird bathrobes sold, as well as the stuffed moosehead with antlers, and a box of 78 phonograph records. Suddenly at two o'clock the jukebox lit up with flashing neon lights and roared out the "Beer Barrel Polka." There were six people in the shop at the time; it was like a party.

All of this increased the momentum I'd returned with from New York, and between sales I began making plans to go to Maine before I lost my courage. I looked up Portland in the atlas, figured routes and mileage and pondered how to handle four or five days away from the shop. The shipment from New York would arrive Wednesday, or Thursday at the latest; I figured that, allowing for one day to price and sort the new items, I could leave for Maine on Saturday morning. I telephoned Mr. Georgerakis and put my proposition to him.

"I thought you'd never ask," he said over the phone. "Today I read the newspaper all morning and after lunch I ran the vacuum cleaner for Katina. This is retirement?"

"How much do you think I should pay you for coming in?" I asked.

"This is not the question of a businesswoman," he told me, "but I appreciate the delicacy. Listen, I'd do it for free but I have my dignity; pay me ten dollars a day but no vacuuming."

"Mr. Georgerakis, I don't even own a vacuum cleaner," I told him.

"God bless you for that, I'll be there Saturday morning eight o'clock sharp. Consider it balm for my soul."

When Joe came at five I wondered why on earth I'd felt so afraid; he wasn't even as handsome as I remembered, just bony and nice-looking, cheerful and somehow very real. "You look good enough to eat," he said. "What was the chap on Park Avenue like?"

"A dirty old man, I think."

Joe grinned. "Innocent Amelia, you are getting around. You handled him skillfully, I trust?"

"I bolted."

"And the actor?"

"Oh, very nice, although we only talked on the stairs. *He* bought the hurdy-gurdy from a cousin, a Miss Harrington, when her estate went on the market. She's in a private psychiatric hospital in Portland. I suppose she could be mad as a hatter, but I have to try."

He nodded. "Definitely, since one person's definition of mad as a hatter is entirely different from another's.

63

Actually," he added, "I've called my sister mad as a hatter any number of times."

"And is she?"

"Oh—absolutely," he said with mock solemnity and reached for my hand as we walked.

We spent the next two hours peering into and under cars, and another hour excitedly discussing them over meatballs and spaghetti, and in the end I owned a van. It was a really weird one; someone had custom ordered it and then walked out on the deal so that the dealer was very accommodating about the price. It was black as a hearse; with a porthole on either side; and on both the sides and the rear were pale blue ovals on which pictures had been painted of a lighthouse in the moonlight, with thin white lines of surf curling around the gray rocks. The effect of ghostly blues and white on black was altogether spooky, but there was no doubt about what the van would hold: an entire room of furniture if necessary.

"This will certainly amuse my parents," Joe said. "But I haven't invited you, have I?"

"Invited me?" I had just unlocked the door of the shop; the bells were still jangling as I reached for the light switch.

With the lights on I saw that Joe was looking pleased with himself. "They're celebrating their thirty-fifth wedding anniversary on Sunday and I told them I'd bring you. You'll come, won't you? If you close the shop in mid-afternoon Saturday we can be there for dinner and they said they'd love meeting you. I can't wait to have you meet them."

I looked at him blankly. "*This* weekend?"

"Right."

"But Joe—"

"What's the matter?"

I looked at him and said, "Joe, I'm leaving for Maine early Saturday morning."

"So soon?" He looked startled. "But that can wait, can't it? What's the rush? You can postpone, can't you?"

I swallowed hard. "I don't—I don't really think I can."

He stared at me incredulously. "But Amelia, this will be fun, damn it. We can go swimming, there's badminton and you'll really enjoy my sister Jenny. You can't be serious."

"But I am," I said helplessly. "When you talk about swimming and badminton I—I can't help it, it just hasn't any reality for me. Going to Maine is something I have to do. I've already made all the arrangements, and Mr. Georgerakis is coming in to look after the shop while I'm gone."

"Amelia," he said in astonishment, "aren't you letting this get out of hand?"

"I'm sorry," I said miserably. "Truly I am."

"Sorry!" he exploded. "My God, here I am with free time at last and I was hoping, I was planning—I thought we really hit it off tremendously well, and damn it Amelia, this woman's dead, she has to be. But I'm not. Look at me, Amelia, I'm alive and I'm here, and it's *summer*."

"I can't help it," I said stubbornly. "I just can't. I have to go to Maine and look for Hannah."

"You think I invite girls home every weekend to meet my parents?" he demanded.

"I don't know."

"You happen to be the first," he said, and we stared at each other across a vast chasm. "I don't get it, I honestly don't get it," he said furiously, "but I hope you enjoy your damn trip very much." Giving me a glance to match his voice he stalked out of the shop and closed the door so hard the bells hanging over it kept clanging and jangling for a full minute.

Well, of course I'd known it would have to happen. I'd really been expecting it, hadn't I? A part of me whispered, 'Hurry—run after him and say you'll go' but I only stood there, feeling numb. This was the thing about people: they either rejected you or they swallowed you up, and you couldn't be your own self. If you tried to be yourself, if you asserted, they went away, which is what my mother had always done to punish me, so why not Joe? I had long ago learned anyway that everything I became attached to either went away, changed, or died. Suddenly all my inadequacies rose in me like vomit. I felt guilt at daring to do what I wanted, bruised at hurting Joe and, worst of all, a crushing fear that I might be losing my mind over what could only be an insane search for a dead woman.

Frightened, I reached for a sweater and locked the door of the shop, knowing that this time I was going to Amman Singh as a supplicant, a beggar of alms. I hadn't seen him for a week; there was so much to tell him and so much I wanted from him. Whatever it was I wanted it badly.

The smell of curry and spices hung in the air outside his door. He was mercifully alone, except for the ubiquitous relatives whom I could hear poking about in the kitchen, talking in low voices. After five flights of stairs I said breathlessly, "Amman Singh, I have to talk to you. Please?"

"I have been expecting you," he said courteously, and gestured me to sit down beside him.

I sat facing him, my legs crossed under me. "I think I have to tell this like a story."

He nodded. "You know I enjoy stories."

I told him about the hurdy-gurdy and about the note I'd found inside of it, and I told him about the people

66

I'd visited and met since I last saw him. Only when I'd finished did I look at him, and I saw that he had closed his eyes to listen. I remembered his saying once that it wasn't just to the words he listened, but to what lay behind them, and I wondered what nuances and inflections he heard in my voice to give away my loneliness, my doubts and my sudden terror. I pleaded, "Amman Singh, why am I doing this? Is it destructive? Am I right to do this?"

"Right?" he repeated. "Right?"

"I don't understand myself, I don't understand this—this need, this compulsion. Hannah surely has to be dead by now."

He was silent for a long time and then he opened his eyes. He reached out for my hand and touched it; his grasp felt dry and cool, scarcely flesh at all. "Please," he said.

"Please what?"

"When the wind frees the seed from the flower," he said, "and the seed is driven on the breeze across the fields it is not compulsion. The seed is obeying laws we cannot see or know. Trust the wind. One day you will understand."

"But will I find her?" I asked.

He said, "You will find something."

"But it's Hannah I must find!" I cried.

He looked at me and his smile was tender. "Is it?" he asked softly. "Is it?"

I felt better after leaving Amman Singh, although I didn't understand what he meant, not then at least. But he had said I would find something, and since I had just lost Joe that was better than nothing. Still, it was astonishing how impoverished and dull my life suddenly looked without Joe. I had thought I'd found a friend. Until now I'd had only one friend, except that

67

I'd never had any illusions about the bond between Shirley Newcomb and me in junior high school. Shirley had been as fat as I was scrawny, and just as unnoticed. We were united only in our envy of cheerleaders, by our invisibility to everyone in our classes, and our penchant for flunking algebra. I'd never brought her home with me; at best it had been a sickly friendship and when, in our freshman year at high school, she and her family moved away it was almost a relief. After all, we'd never had anything in common but our deficiencies. It seemed kinder to face loneliness alone.

But a grayness, a lack of sun, hung over everything like smog the next day. I tried to go back in time to my life before I met Joe; I tried reliving my gratitude at finding the Ebbtide Shop, and my excitement over buying it, but Joe stood there like a wall, dividing the two worlds. Finding Hannah's note in the hurdy-gurdy had brought him into my life and now, with equal dispatch, it had removed him. How treacherous fate was!

On Wednesday afternoon the truck brought my goods from New York and in a fury of work I rearranged the shop's window display, and then I stayed up until midnight painting the last wall of the shop, which I'd been too busy to finish a month ago. I draped a few lengths of the Indian fabric across one wall in a great colorful swath, laid out the blue willow ware, and hung price tags on the line of cuckoo clocks.

On Thursday, after dinner, I dialed Joe's telephone number just to hear his voice, planning to hang up as soon as he answered. I was denied even that: there was no answer. I called again at midnight, out of some perverse anger, and still there was no answer. Obviously he was finding solace elsewhere: a woman, I thought darkly, and one more amenable than I.

Not entirely sure what "amenable" really meant I looked it up in the dictionary and found that it meant

Hannah's note three times before my sense of mission was restored and my anxieties banished; my safety zones were being pounded against rocks by a heavy surf. I packed blue jeans, a heavy turtleneck sweater, my windbreaker, pajamas, and toothbrush, and at eight o'clock in the morning I greeted Mr. Georgerakis wearing my ubiquitous beige corduroy suit, this time enlivened by a pink and orange scarf. Half an hour later when I carried my suitcase out to the alley where the van was parked at night I stopped dead in my tracks in shock. Joe was leaning against the side of the van.

"Hi," he said cheerfully. "If you'd only left this monster of yours unlocked I'd have stowed away and shouted 'boo' to you along about Massachusetts. But you locked the darn thing, and anyway I'd have only scared you to death and killed us both."

I stared at him, not understanding a single word he said.

Fortunately he chose to be more explicit. "I'm going with you to Maine," he said, pointing to a dufflebag at his feet that I hadn't noticed in my shock. "Unless you mind?"

"Mind!" I gasped. "But your parents!"

He said with a shrug, "No problem. I drove down Wednesday to wish them another thirty-five years of connubial bliss and got back last night. Told them I just couldn't make it over the weekend for the big event."

I must have looked as dazed as I felt—after all, I'd lost him, attended the funeral services, mourned him and buried him by now—because he added patiently, "Look, Amelia, if Hannah's top priority for you right now I'll make her mine, too, but only for a little while, you understand? For that matter I may have to be back here Wednesday for a court case but I'm yours until then. I think this is what's called compromise."

I could have told him that it was also generosity but I only grinned from ear to ear and said, "I'm so awfully glad to see you, Joe. Would you like to drive first, or shall I?"

PART II

"Beware all greedy men, Colin, for who knows where they will stop? If they envy you your fine pendant of jade and feathers, who's to know if they will bargain for it, snatch it, or kill you?"

The Magistrate, in *The Maze in the Heart of the Castle*

6

There was no Greenwood Hospital in Portland but there was a private psychiatric hospital five miles out of town called Greenacres. It was a gently aging building of rosy brick surrounded by improbably green lawns, like Astroturf, except that they had to be real because a man was mowing to the south of the building. I swung the van into the parking space labeled VISITORS ONLY and turned off the ignition. "So," I said brightly, "we're here."

"We're here, and it's all yours," Joe reminded me, pointedly bringing out his paperback copy of *Astronomy for the Layman*. "Good luck, bon voyage and all that."

He said the last very dryly because we'd talked and

argued for several hours about how I was going to get inside to see Leonora Harrington if she was here; we'd phoned to learn the Sunday visiting hours but we'd not dared ask if she was a patient. It was Joe's theory that in any private hospital, considering its astonomical costs, no one was going to allow a presumptuous and impertinent young stranger to bother a patient without a darn good reason. Unfortunately neither of us had been able to think of one.

And so it was up to me. Naturally.

I walked up the wide, shallow cement steps to the huge door, half wood, half glass. Looking in before I entered I could see that it looked just like any hospital: there was a brightly lighted reception counter on the left, with clipboards and a switchboard, and a waiting room on the right. The only difference was that the reception counter was Italian marble and mahogany, and the waiting room was done in shades of mauve, purple and pink. Sunday visiting hours began at two o'clock, and since it was now two-ten the waiting room was empty, the only person in sight a nurse in very starched white behind the counter. She looked young, earnest, and new.

I said politely, "Good afternoon, I've come to see Miss Leonora Harrington if she's receiving visitors today."

The girl's friendly smile turned startled. *"Miss Harrington?"*

"Yes. Unless of course she's—"

"Oh no, it's just she never has—" The girl stopped, flushed, and began again. "That is, usually no one except—I'll have to check it out, would you mind waiting a minute?"

She was even more inarticulate than I at my worst.

A very severe-looking middle-aged nurse was produced next, who proved to be more articulate. "I'm Mrs.

76

Dawes," she announced. "Are you a member of Miss Harrington's family?"

Hers was the cold voice of authority, and her gaze was sharp enough to strip a person of pretensions, illusions, and confidence. I am very familiar with the type: they like helpless people and rendering people helpless, and I saw no reason to frustrate her. "Oh I do so hope I can see her for just a minute," I said, turning arch, naïve, and awkward. "I have no right, of course—not at all—but her cousin Robert Lamandale in New York referred me here. It's a legal matter," I added, gesturing helplessly. "It's so important that she identify this photograph of a hurdy-gurdy."

This floored her. "A *what*?"

I produced the snapshots and placed them on the counter. "I wouldn't for the world want to be a bother and of course you've every right—"

I've noticed that if someone is about to tell you that you've no right to do something it confuses them no end if you say it first. The hurdy-gurdy confused her, too; I mean, it had the unexpectedness of a *non sequitur*. I do not mean to imply that Mrs. Dawes warmed to me but she blinked, and her gaze changed in quality from flint to steel. "You do know Mr. Lamandale then," she said.

"Yes. Robert Lamandale, in New York. The actor."

"Dr. Ffolks is in his office," she said coldly. "I really don't know—"

No one seemed to finish their sentences here, but I was content; I often don't finish them myself. I stood there trying to look poised, since I was here on a legal matter, and at the same time helpless, to placate Nurse Dawes. It was a difficult combination. Presently a man in a white coat accompanied Mrs. Dawes down the hall to inspect me. He looked very tired and all the lines in his face sagged, including his jowls, which gave him an uncanny resemblance to a St. Bernard dog. He nodded to me curtly. "Nurse Jordan will of course have to accompany you for the visit," he said, "and it will have to be limited to five minutes. Miss Harrington's under sedation but she's quite lucid. Miss Jordan?"

"Yes, Dr. Ffolks," said the young nurse. "This way, miss."

I was glad I'd decided on the truth since I was to have a witness to my interview. Both Dr. Ffolks and Mrs. Dawes stood and watched us walk to the elevator and then lingered to eavesdrop frankly while we waited for its arrival. I commented breathlessly to Nurse Jordan on the signs of spring in Maine, the greenness of the lawn outside, and then we stepped into the elevator and at once I stopped such nonsense and asked how long Miss Harrington had lived at Greenacres.

"Oh, practically forever," said Nurse Jordan cheerfully. "She was here when my mum worked nights, and that was eight years ago when we were all kids."

"Weird," I said, and we exchanged the knowing glances of contemporaries.

"They say she drank all her money away," Nurse Jordan added in a lowered voice as the elevator slowed. "They say she's paranoid, too, but I've never—"

The doors slid open soundlessly at the third floor and we stepped out on a corridor with windows at either end. Miss Jordan knocked on the door opposite the elevator, opened it, and I followed her into a room with its curtains half drawn against the sunlight.

"I didn't ring," said a petulant voice from the left-hand corner of the room, "and if you dare to say are we having one of our bad days I'll throw a glass of water at you."

"But I've brought you a guest," Nurse Jordan said in a neutral, colorless voice.

In the bed along the left wall of the room a woman stirred, sat up, and peered at me. Adjusting to the semi-darkness I could see her now. It was hard to guess how old she was, she could have been thirty or forty; her face was an oval from which all emotion and life had been drained. Only her eyes were alive, and they burned like the eyes of someone who looked frequently into hell. She must have been beautiful once, one of those fragile and very exquisite ash blondes; the bone structure was still there. Her hair, striped now with gray, hung to her shoulders but it looked as if she ran her fingers through it often, and with anger. Seeing me she tilted her head questioningly.

"This is Miss Jones," said Nurse Jordan. "She's a friend of your cousin, come to see you. Your cousin in New York."

Miss Harrington's face brightened. She said eagerly, "Robin? You've seen Robin?"

Robin. I was so startled I almost jumped. Robin—and her name was Leonora. Of course—Robin and Nora! It was like panning for gold and suddenly bringing up a fortune-sized nugget; I found it hard to suppress my excitement but I said calmly, "Yes, and he's just auditioned for a part in an important play in New York. He sent his best to you, and he said it was all right to ask you about this."

I placed the two pictures of the hurdy-gurdy on her bed table. She turned on the bedside light and leaned over to peer at them.

"Oh my God," she said softly, tears coming to her eyes. "Oh my God, Aunt Hannah's hurdy-gurdy. How we loved it as children!"

"Your aunt Hannah," I repeated carefully, really excited now but not wanting to frighten her. Matching the softness of her voice I added, "Was her name Harrington, too?"

But she was staring at the snapshots, bemused, the tears sliding down her haggard cheeks and splotching the pictures.

"Your cousin Robin said that it was your hurdy-gurdy later, that *you* owned it for a while," I pointed out. "Is that true? I'm trying to trace it, you see. It *was* yours at one time?"

She nodded. "I kept it ... I chose it ... as a souvenir, you know—after everything went. Everything. Oh, I hated selling it but I needed the money," she said with sudden anger.

I said quickly, aware of my limited time with her, "Where did you and Robin play with the hurdy-gurdy, Miss Harrington? I mean, where did your aunt live?"

"In Carleton."

"Carleton, Maine?"

She nodded absently; her eyes were looking far beyond the pictures into a past she'd lost.

"And your aunt Hannah's last name, was it Harrington, too? Or perhaps Lamandale?"

She wrenched her gaze from the pictures and stared at me in astonishment. "Of course not—Hannah Meerloo. Why didn't you know that?" she asked suspiciously. "She ought to have known that," she told the nurse pettishly. "I don't like her, I don't like her asking me questions and making me cry. Take her away or I'll call Dr. Ffolks."

Nurse Jordan touched my arm, and as I followed her out of the room, Leonora Harrington called after us spitefully, "Tell Robin to come himself next time, damn him, I'm not insane, you know."

"She'll cry now and fall asleep," Nurse Jordan said as we walked into the elevator and she pressed the L button. "No harm done. She's not always this way. Tomorrow she'll be sitting out on the rear lawn knitting in the sun with all the other patients."

I said, "But if she's so poor, how on earth can she afford to stay here at Greenacres?"

"Oh, a friend of the family pays her bills," explained the nurse. "He's the only one who comes to see her, which is why you surprised me. He comes once a month, regular as clockwork."

The doors slid open and there was Mrs. Dawes waiting for us like a vulture. "Very good," she said, nodding to Nurse Jordan. "Five minutes to the second." Her eyes rested on me dismissingly. "*Good* day, Miss Jones."

I walked alone up the hall to the lobby, and being alone now I suddenly saw what I should have noticed before, except that it would have been meaningless ten minutes earlier. There was a bronze plaque set into the wall in the lobby. It read:

GREENACRES PRIVATE HOSPITAL
Given in memory
OF
JASON M. MEERLOO
BY
HANNAH G. MEERLOO

I walked thoughtfully back to the van, and to Joe, who looked at me questioningly and put aside his book. "That didn't take long. Amelia, you look funny."

I said slowly, "I seem to have found Hannah. Of course not really, but Leonora Harrington is Nora— she has to be—because she called Robert Lamandale *Robin,* and the hurdy-gurdy belonged to their Aunt Hannah, whose last name was Meerloo, and this hospital is the gift of Hannah Meerloo."

"Wow—paydirt," Joe said, and whistled. "And so?"

"I don't know, except that Hannah lived in Carleton, Maine."

"You look scared," he said, looking me over with a professional eye.

I nodded. "Suddenly I know her name now and I don't—don't know what to do with or about it."

Joe grinned. "Then it's a darn good thing I came along because I know exactly what to do. Climb in and I'll drive. We'll look up Carleton on the map and while we drive there you can tell me word for word what happened. What you're suffering from is shock but you'll get over it."

"Joe, you're nice."

"Of course," he said blithely. "Uncannily intelligent as well, and suddenly intrigued by this damnfool hunt of yours, I don't know why."

"I'm not," I said in a small dismayed voice. "I suddenly want to go home."

"That's because you're afraid of success," he said forgivingly. "Lack of confidence and all that. A temporary aberration."

"She doesn't sound like—I didn't realize she'd be rich."

"The rich are human, too, and the rich get murdered, Amelia. Most murders are done for love, money, or revenge. The important thing is to remember her note."

He was right, of course. I was forgetting Hannah's note, I was feeling betrayed by superficialities and facts and unpleasant people and—I had to confess—a meeting with reality. But in her note Hannah had spoken to me, don't ask me why I felt this so deeply because I was only just learning to trust my instincts, but her note was real, and Hannah was real, and it was this I had to hang onto, forgetting petulant nieces and plaques in lobbies.

I looked up Carleton on the road map and found it to the north, on one of the bays or harbors that scallop the Maine coast. "It looks a long way from Portland,"

I said doubtfully. "Maybe a hundred miles up Route 1, and then out on a peninsula." I turned to the back of the map and read aloud, "Its population is 463."

"Then someone will certainly remember a woman named Hannah Meerloo," pointed out Joe. "What's the nearest decent-sized town?"

"There's only one—goodness what a strange state Maine is! Angleworth's the nearest city and *its* population is only 4,687."

Joe turned onto Route 1 and glanced at his watch. "We'll head for Angleworth, it's nearly half-past two already."

I could guess what he was thinking: last night we'd stayed at a modest inn and had quite casually and naturally taken rooms at opposite ends of the building: Miss A. Jones, Mr. J. Osbourne. But that was New Hampshire. Nothing much was open at this season in Maine, and the smaller the towns, the more limited the accommodations. Soon we would have to become self-conscious about what lay between us, which was something that had not occurred to me until we'd crossed the Tappan Zee Bridge in New York State yesterday: was Joe expecting me to sleep with him?

Oddly enough for a virgin it was the word *expect* that terrified me. *Amelia,* my mother used to say sternly, *courtesy means doing the right thing, courtesy is performing graciously what is expected of one.* It sounded like a transaction . . . courtesy for courtesy, and Joe had certainly been kind to come with me to Maine. I did not labor under the illusion that my mother had intended extending one's largesse in this sort of situation but the words were nevertheless engraved on my psyche; expectations had always been heaped upon me and were always my downfall. I realized with a sinking heart that if Joe expected this of me then I would probably sacrifice myself like one of those Mayan or Aztec maidens who leaped off cliffs to appease the gods, or had they immolated themselves instead? I couldn't even remember which it was, having been a dismal student, which was one more expectation I'd botched. I knew I'd botch this, too, if the occasion arose.

"Actually," said Joe, pointing to still another motel with a CLOSED UNTIL MEMORIAL DAY sign, "we haven't any idea what we'll be getting into, Amelia. I think we should stop at L. L. Bean's in Freeport and pick up some camping gear just in case. I brought a sleeping bag but you didn't, and we may have to use the van." His voice was so impersonal—like Peary planning a trip to the North Pole—that I couldn't help but relax.

"Good idea," I said briskly.

They were having a parade in Freeport on this Sunday afternoon, with a high school band that marched along briskly, playing "Strike Up the Band" a little off-key, and a procession of men and women carrying placards that read VOTE FOR ANGUS TUTTLE FOR U.S. SENATOR. A small, amiable group followed the parade on the sidewalk bearing signs reading SILAS WHITNEY FOR U.S. SENATOR. There were a few balloons and friendly shouts but the only excitement seemed to be caused by the traffic jam, until the band disappeared down a side street and we were able to park and walk into L. L. Bean's. Whereupon I proceeded to acquire my first sleeping bag, as well as a pair of hiking boots, a flashlight, thermos, and collapsible drinking cup. I literally had to be dragged out of the store by Joe.

Hours later we stopped in Anglesworth for a quick dinner, had the thermos filled with hot cocoa, and headed immediately for Carleton so that we would reach it before the general store closed. That, Joe said, was the place to learn anything in the country, and he was right. There were two gas pumps and a faded sign saying PRITCHETT'S GENERAL STORE, Simon Pritchett,

Proprietor. Featured in the left-hand window was a placard reading VOTE FOR SILAS WHITNEY, in the right-hand window a sign reading VOTE FOR ANGUS TUTTLE: evenly distributed among these were hand-lettered signs of Grange dinners, bookmobile dates, and town-hall meetings. We walked inside and found Simon Pritchett, proprietor, reading a newspaper behind the counter and the store otherwise deserted. He put aside his newspaper and walked toward us: we met at the pot-bellied stove in the middle of the room, which was engulfed by trade goods of the most incredible variety: boxes of towels and washcloths, snow boots and sleds hanging from the ceiling, blankets and shirts and sou'westers piled high, all of this crowded around a soda cooler, a penny candy counter, and a meat locker. Joe gave the man a pleasant smile and said, "Good evening."

"'Evening," said the man, "can I help you folks?"

"We're hoping you can," Joe told him. "My friend here, Amelia Jones, is looking for the place where Mrs. Hannah Meerloo used to live."

"A very dear friend of my family's at one time," I added, seeing him look at me with a sharpened, warier glance.

He was silent, mulling us over thoughtfully for a long minute. He must have decided at last that we were trustworthy because he finally nodded and said, "That'd be the place up for sale again by the summer folks who bought it three years ago. The Keppel place."

"Keppel," I repeated.

He nodded. "Down the road a piece, far as the fork. Bear to the right—that'd be Tuttle Road—and you'll find it on your left, near the river. Big place, can't miss the for sale sign on the white brick wall." Having spewed this out he looked at me expectantly, obviously waiting to learn what I was going to do with a closed-

85

up house behind a white brick wall. I asked instead with a smile, "Did you know Hannah Meerloo?"

"Know everyone in Carleton," he said cautiously. "One time or 'nother."

"She—uh—died . . . I mean, of course she's dead but—?"

I stopped doubtfully.

"Buried in the town cemetery," he said flatly. "Can't be deader than that."

So that was that.

Joe, seeing the expression on my face, stepped into the breach to ask casually, "And for how long did she happen to live in Carleton, do you recall?"

"Fifteen, maybe eighteen years. She warn't no summer resident," he said with the contempt of a native in his voice for those who came only during the golden months. With a curious glance he added, "You one of these people tracing roots I hear about?"

"Something like that," Joe said easily. "How much would half a dozen of these all-day suckers cost? And perhaps you could also direct us to the town cemetery?"

"Fifty cents plus tax, and the cemetery's just across the road behind the Methodist church," he said, leaving me awed by Joe's clear thinking. No need to ask how long ago she'd died; the cemetery would tell us.

And so at dusk on a warm May evening we wandered through the Carleton cemetery in search of Hannah's grave. It was a good cemetery, well-kept, with carefully weeded mounds punctuated by modest upright granite slabs, dozens of them in neat rows reaching back centuries. The sun was low and turned the grass a brilliant emerald green as it slanted through the huge old trees. Woven into the hushed silence were a few bird calls and the steady snip-snip of grass shears wielded by a boy at the far end of the cemetery. We strolled over to ask him if he could tell us where the Meerloo plot was, and after a moment's thought he pointed.

And there it was, except there were two stones, very simple ones, side by side. The stone on the left read:

JASON M. MEERLOO
b. January 23, 1920—killed in France
December, 1945

"Good grief," I said, "he was only twenty-five, do you suppose he was husband or brother?"

Joe pointed wordlessly to the bottom words, nearly covered by the ivy trailing over the stone. They read, BELOVED HUSBAND OF HANNAH.

"Husband," I said automatically. The sun had withdrawn now and it was nearly dark among the trees. As I knelt beside the companion gravestone I switched on my flashlight.

"HANNAH G. MEERLOO," I read softly. "Born May 27, 1925, died July 25, 1965 . . ." *So long ago,* I thought, startled, and then I subtracted one date from another and said, "Joe, she was only forty."

Joe was doing sums in his head, too. "It also means," he said, "that when she was widowed in 1945 she was twenty-one years old. Younger than you are now, Amelia."

But I was staring at the inscription below the dates and the name. Puzzled, I leaned closer with my flashlight and pushed aside a tendril of ivy to make certain I was reading the inscription correctly, for below the date of her death were the words . . . *and so she went beyond the horizon into the country of the dawn* . . .

Strange words . . . strange and poetic and somehow familiar to me. "That's surely a quotation," I told Joe, concentrating the beam of light on the words and frowning over them. "Is it familiar to you?"

He shook his head. "I like it, though. I think it means—" He hesitated and then he said very quietly, "I think it means there was someone left behind who loved her."

It was at that moment, hearing him say that, and in that kind of voice, that I believe I fell in love with Joe. *And so she went beyond the horizon into the country of the dawn* ... Puzzling. Puzzling and somehow very personal and loving, exactly as Joe pointed out.

"Come on," Joe said, putting a hand on my shoulder. "It's dark and getting cold and it's nearly eight o'clock. I think it's time we find a place to park the van, have some cocoa and turn in. I'm beat, myself."

I turned and looked up at him and I said urgently, "But there'll be records, won't there, Joe? Newspapers keep records, don't they? And a death certificate somewhere?"

"Tomorrow," he said. "Tomorrow, Amelia." And he helped me to my feet and firmly led me away from the grave.

We found a deserted wood road, drank our cocoa and curled up in our sleeping bags inside the van, Joe on one side, and I on the other. I fell asleep at once, tired from two days of driving, waiting, and tension. I must have been asleep for several hours when it began again.... I was wandering through long empty cold halls, calling "Mother?" and looking into cold empty rooms, and then I was slowly climbing the attic stairs—slowly, slowly, as one does in a dream—and there she was at the top of the stairs, hanging from a rafter, turning, gently turning and swaying, my mother and yet not my mother, her face swollen and suffused, her eyes—

I screamed, and screamed again, and—waking—opened my eyes to find the flashlight switched on and Joe struggling out of his sleeping bag. "My God, Amelia," he said. "What is it?"

I had long ago stopped crying following this nightmare but as usual I was shaking all over. "My God, Amelia," Joe repeated, staring at me, and he put his arms around me and held me.

When I'd stopped shaking I said, "I had a nightmare."

"So I gathered," he said dryly. "Talk it out. It helps, you know."

Through clenched teeth I said, "When I was eleven my mother didn't just die, as I told you. She hung herself. And always—always when I have these nightmares—I see her. See her hanging there, her neck broken and—"

He said incredulously, "She hung herself and *you found her*?"

"Yes."

"And you were eleven years old?"

I nodded.

"My God," he said with a shudder. "And you've had to live with this ever since?"

"I'm all right now," I told him. "I think you can go to sleep again now, I'm feeling better. It's over."

"What do you mean it's 'over'?" he demanded. "Don't be polite, Amelia. Have some cocoa. It won't be warm but there's some left in the bottom of the thermos." He began rummaging about for the cup, the flashlight sending long cavernous shadows caroming up and down the walls of the van. He said, "Have you ever learned *why* your mother committed suicide?"

I said politely, "Well—she gave up, of course. On living, I mean."

"Yes, but she had an eleven-year-old daughter and

a husband, didn't she? What kind of woman would be so careless about *them*?" he asked, bringing me the cocoa in a cup.

I said dryly, "A woman with an infinite lack of capacity for living."

"Were you close to her?"

I thought about this while I sipped the cocoa. "Of course I wanted to be close to her but there always seemed such a high price to pay. Dr. Merivale said she looked on me as an extension of herself. Myself, I think when I was born she thought, 'Ah—at last someone to give me unqualified and total love.'"

"Quite a lot to ask of a just-born infant," snorted Joe.

"I know," I said sadly. "As it turned out, nothing I did was right because nothing I could do was enough."

"Then what she wanted—surely—was total possession?"

"Perhaps," I admitted. "There was—apparently," I added loyally, "some tragedy in her life."

"There's tragedy in everyone's life, Amelia," he said sternly.

"Because," I continued, "just before the funeral I heard my father and my aunt Stacey talking in the living room. I wasn't supposed to hear, I was sitting on the stairs listening to them. I heard my father tell my aunt Stacey that my mother had never loved him, that he'd given up years ago trying to reach her, that she'd never stopped loving someone named Charles who rejected her and married someone else. She never stopped mourning him."

"Did she try?" asked Joe savagely.

I laughed in a hollow sort of way. "Not very hard, no. I think now, looking back, she had been in love with death for a long time. She liked graveyards, you see. I remember when I was very young, before I went to school, we used to visit them often. Not for stone-rubbing or collecting epitaphs but just to walk through them, and she'd stop and say to me in a special dreamy sort of voice, 'Just think, Amelia, all the people here were once alive, just like you and me, and one day we, too—.' She'd never finish the sentence but she made her point. Life, she would say with a sigh, was so very brief. And I guess she found it very pointless."

Joe said harshly, "It sounds to me as if she suffered from an orgy of Victorian melancholia. Didn't your father know or care what she was doing to you?"

"He was away a lot."

"Was he away the day she hung herself?"

"Oh yes."

"So your mother knew you'd find her?"

I looked at him sharply. "Why do you say that?" I asked angrily.

"Because," he pointed out simply, "if she knew you would be the one to find her, it was the ultimate rejection for you. The ultimate abandonment."

The ultimate rejection . . . no one had ever put it in that way before, so bluntly, so honestly, with such a knife-edge clarity, but of course that was it, that was what had always mattered far more to me than finding her dead.

"The ultimate punishment, too," I added quietly, "for not being enough to her." And suddenly the tears I'd not cried for so long overwhelmed me and I sobbed in Joe's arms, and gulped and sobbed some more, and finally, reduced to hiccups, I sat up and looked at him, finding him blurred through my lingering tears, and I smiled at him. "Thanks," I said. "I needed that."

He laughed. "You're going to be all right, you know—that's the thing to remember, Amelia. In my book you're already okay. The absence of love is very prevalent in this world, and the word love is the most

91

corrupted word in the dictionary. But patterns can be broken, you know."

"I sure hope so," I said, and softly quoted Amman Singh. "A tree may be bent by harsh winds but is no less beautiful than the tree that grows in a sheltered nook, and often it bears the richer fruit...."

He stared at me gravely in the light of the torch beside us. "You're a very lovely, special sort of person, Amelia, do you know that?"

I looked at him, startled, and then—flippantly, gratefully—I leaned over and kissed him, except that when our lips met our arms somehow curved instantly, greedily, around each other and suddenly there was nothing of gratitude in the strange wild heat that rose in me. I gasped, "Joe—"

He said questioningly, almost desperately, "Amelia—" and a moment later we were inside my sleeping bag, our clothes strewn across the floor and I was learning for the first time the new and exotic language of the body and there was nothing sacrificial about me at all.

Thus was I deflowered, as the Victorians would say. Delightfully, lustily, willingly, and with much pleasure, in a black van with portholes in Carleton, Maine. No Aztec maiden, I.

Later, smoothing my tangled hair, Joe said, "Let's never be careless with each other, Amelia, promise? Because what happened just now between us is too important."

"Yes," I said dreamily, "but when can it happen again, Joe?"

He laughed. "Go to sleep, you wanton child."

I giggled and closed my eyes and lay there, feeling the warmth of his body next to mine—how amazing life could be, after all!—and knowing that when we woke up we'd make love again. It was almost enough to make me forget Hannah, the Hannah who *went beyond the horizon into the country of the dawn.*

And suddenly, just as I was slipping into a grateful sleep, I remembered the source of the quotation: it surfaced smoothly into consciousness, striking me full force, like a blast of lightning, so that I wondered how I could have missed it earlier. Except for the change in gender it was a word-for-word quotation from *The Maze in the Heart of the Castle.* They were the closing lines of the book: *and so he went beyond the horizon into the country of the dawn.*

7

"She must have loved the book, too," I told Joe incredulously the next morning at breakfast. We were seated at a diner in Anglesworth and it was ten o'clock. "I mean, it's been out of print for years. It's the most astonishing thing."

"I've never heard of *The Maze in the Heart of the Castle*," Joe said, biting into his toast. "Are you certain the inscription on the gravestone is the same? It must be years since you've read it."

"But it isn't," I told him eagerly. "I mean, besides rereading it once a year I bought a first edition of it in New York only last week. I would have shown it to you if you—if we—well, anyway, I found it in a secondhand bookstore and although I only thumbed through it I reread that same last page before I put it away . . . *and so he went beyond the horizon into the country of the dawn*."

"The book meant that much to you?"

"It saved my life," I told him earnestly. "I was so very young, you know, and so clobbered. It gave me a kind of philosophy."

"And what was it?" Joe asked, smiling faintly as he watched me.

I considered this because, after all, what *had* it given me besides entertainment? "It gave me a certain *feeling*," I said, choosing words cautiously, "and out of this feeling came the idea that maybe life isn't meant to be easy, that it's a kind of pilgrimage or testing ground, and we have to fight like warriors to live. I mean to live *well*."

"Like warriors," Joe repeated, sounding interested.

"But that isn't right, either," I said despairingly. "Oh I wish I'd brought the book with me so you could see for yourself. It's a wonderful book, Joe, he meets the Despas and the Wos and the Conjurer and then the Talmars, and he escapes them to meet the Magistrate and then falls in love with a girl named Charmian, who betrays him, and finally he meets Serena—oh yes and Raoul, too, who's Prince of Galt, and once he's reached the Galts, you see, he's gone through the maze, he's free, and he and Serena . . ." I trailed off limply. "Well, I do wish you could know what I'm talking about."

"I'm admiring you while you describe it," Joe said, grinning. "How did you come by the book?"

I remembered that clearly. "My aunt Stacey sent it to me for Christmas just after Mother died."

"So the book was published eleven or twelve years ago?"

I shook my head. "It wasn't a new book when she sent it, which surprised me, because Aunt Stacey lived on the West Coast and usually sent new, glamorous, California-type presents. I thought at the time it might have been one of her books when she was young, except that the book was published in 1949 or 1950, I forget which. She must have bought it in a secondhand store because she'd heard something about it, or thought I'd like it."

"As you certainly did," said Joe.

I nodded and said solemnly, "I think I like this Hannah of ours very much, Joe."

Joe brought me down from my trip by saying, "It's certainly convenient you like her, but we're here to establish whether she was murdered or not, remember? And it's Monday morning, and sometime today I'm going to have to call my answering service—"

I was impressed. "You have an *answering* service, Joe?"

"—and see whether there are any messages about being in court Wednesday. Yes I have an answering service."

"What happens Wednesday?" I asked. On Saturday morning Wednesday had seemed a century away; now it loomed closer, it had a shape to it, it was something that could remove Joe, and I was feeling less charitable.

"It's when Griselda's case may or may not come to court," he said. "Griselda's eleven years old and was taken away from her grandmother because her grandmother's seventy-three and can't jump rope with her, for heaven's sake. She was put in a foster home where she changed so much over a period of two years that they've decided she's schizophrenic and ought to be institutionalized."

"Oboy," I said.

He nodded. "Her grandmother's a smart cookie and

hired a lawyer, who hired me. We've collected handwriting samples from years back, and think we can prove 1) that the foster parents are the crazies and 2) that Griselda has withdrawn because she has niether stability nor love in her life. She needs her grandmother."

"Will there be someone to believe you?" I asked cautiously.

"One always hopes," he said. "There'll be some heavy batteries drawn up against us, because bureaucracies are certainly not happy about being wrong, which is why they're playing games with us about the court hearing." He drank the last of his coffee and put the cup down. "Are you finished yet? We've got a long list of things to do today, Amelia."

"Right," I said, and swallowed the last of my toast. "Death certificate first, or obituaries?"

"I think death certificate first," Joe said. "After all, if it turns out that Hannah died in a hospital of pneumonia, or collapsed of a heart attack in full view of a crowd of people, then we might as well go sightseeing."

"Joe, you don't really think—"

"Verify, Amelia, verify," he said with a grin. "Don't forget I have a lawyer for a father, and some of his legal mind has rubbed off on me. Verify *everything*."

It was a shabby diner, with an eroded mirror behind the counter. While Joe paid the bill and asked directions to the courthouse I studied its dreary decorations, which consisted mainly of signs pasted over the scars across the huge mirror: IN GOD WE TRUST BUT NOT IN CREDIT; A SMILE COSTS NOTHING, TRY IT, and the same ubiquitous political posters, which this time I read in depth: FOR U.S. SENATOR ELECT ANGUS TUTTLE, *four years State Senator, a man of experience, a man of vision.* This poster carried a photograph of him wearing tweeds and sitting in an armchair looking like a man

97

in a toothpaste ad. He had prematurely white hair, handsome brows, a young face, and that broad, dazzling white smile.

The other poster read VOTE FOR SILAS WHITNEY FOR U.S. SENATE, *a man of the people, a new voice, a man of judgment*. There was a picture of him, too; he looked as if his face had been carved out of granite, long and thin, with long thin lines running from nose to mouth, steady black eyes and a lantern jaw. Silas Whitney looked as if he really did have judgment and was a man of the people but I guessed he was already doomed. I didn't think he had a chance against that enormous toothy smile.

"What on earth are you doing?" asked Joe, seeing my lips moving silently.

"Counting teeth," I said, pointing to Tuttle's political poster. "His smile shows twelve upper teeth, it's unbelievable."

"So are you," he said, reaching for my hand, and as we walked out into the sunshine Joe looked down and smiled at me. It was a lovely smile, made up of all that we'd shared together since we awoke at six that morning in each other's arms, and I couldn't help wondering if I'd ever be so happy again. I think I realized even then that it was real, but that it wasn't real like work and morning and eating and sleeping, and that enchanted moments come seldom, like beads on a long string with spaces in between. But this made it all the more precious; I had never been cherished before, or truly and utterly happy.

The courthouse stood on a side street, a very old building with Corinthian columns and a fine frieze set into the inverted V over the entrance. We had to ask, and then look for the City Clerk's office, and then it was necessary to buy a copy of the death certificate in order to see it. "It's how they make a little money," Joe pointed out, amused at my indignation.

But I wasn't really indignant at buying it. I was trembling with suspense and angry at the wait. This was the moment of truth: if, as Joe had pointed out, Hannah had died of pneumonia or a heart attack, then how was I going to reconcile it with the note in the hurdy-gurdy? Was I about to discover that I had been a fool to take the note so seriously, after all I'd gone through to find Hannah?

The copy of the death certificate was presented to us, I paid the two dollars and we leaned over it eagerly, my eyes skidding past the name MEERLOO and down to the cause of death: *a*, it read, *intracranial hemorrhage; b, basalar skull fracture*. It was signed by Timothy Cox, M.D.

"*Not* pneumonia," I said flatly. "*Not* heart attack."

Joe shook his head. "Skull fracture."

"Like maybe a blow on the head," I said. "Joe, let's get to the newspaper office and see if we can find an obituary."

He nodded, and it surprised me how startled he looked. I suppose until now his interest had been spasmodic and academic and the thought of foul play unreal; he had come along only for the ride, so to speak, and to humor me. Now his attention had been wrenched away from me—I didn't begrudge it for a moment—and was fastened upon five words on a certificate that couldn't be lightly explained away by anyone who had read Hannah's note. The possibility of a murder was just becoming real to Joe for the first time, I could actually see it happening.

The Anglesworth newspaper was on the main street, and its office so small that I was afraid they might not have files of back issues; but I was wrong: the office was small but its basement ran under all the other shops in the building.

"You might as well come down with me if you're doing some kind of research," the woman clerk told us. "It's a bit clammy down there but there's a table for reading, and chairs; 1965, you said?"

"July 25, 1965," I reminded her.

"Well, that's easy enough, we've only microfilmed up to 1963. The newspaper," she added in a pleased voice, "was founded in 1897."

The Anglesworth *Tribune* was a weekly paper, which was disappointing, but it explained why the plastic-bound volume for 1965 could be easily carried to the table and deposited there by one person. The clerk went upstairs, and Joe and I eagerly opened the looseleaf jacket and riffled through the pages to May.

"Obituaries, obituaries," I murmured, running my finger down the index on the first page of the July 28 issue.

Joe said in a strange voice, "You don't have to look for the obituaries, Amelia."

I followed his pointing finger to the headline on the first page of the *Tribune:* NOTED RESIDENT DIES IN BI-ZARRE ACCIDENT.

"Bizarre accident," I repeated aloud. "Joe, it says bizarre accident. *They must have gotten away with it*."

And then I saw the subheadline: "Hannah Gruble Meerloo, Philanthropist and Author, Dead at 40."

My eyes were caught—trapped—by the word author and the word Gruble. Only with an effort did I wrench them free to skim the page, my heart literally pounding, my breath suspended . . . and there it was, down near the end of the column: *"in 1950 Mrs. Meerloo, using her maiden name of Gruble, published a book for young people entitled 'The Maze in the Heart of the Castle,' of which the New York* Times *wrote, 'a small classic,*

100

a book for adults as well as children, full of enchant-
ments and insights.' It is the only book Mrs. Meerloo is
known to have written."

I whispered, "Joe, she's H. M. Gruble—*my* Gruble.
She *wrote* the book."

"Take it easy for heaven's sake," Joe said. "You look
as if you're going to faint, Amelia. Are you all right?"

I just stared at him, my head spinning. No, not my
head but the thoughts inside of it...*and so she went
beyond the horizon into the country of the dawn....If
search you must then I can only give you this advice,
the important thing is to carry the sun with you, because
there will be a great and terrifying darkness...But I
must clear up one detail, my dear young lady, that is
not a hurdy-gurdy but a mere hand organ...They're
going to kill me soon—in a few hours I think...Look,
whoever this is, she has to be dead now, which makes
you some kind of a nut, doesn't it?* and Amman Singh
saying to me, *Trust the wind. Someday you will understand.*

I said in a clear hard voice, "I am very much all
right, Joe, I am very *much* all right."

And I sat down at the table, glanced politely at a
rather blurred photograph of a woman that capped the
story, and began to carefully read the column below it.

July 25/ Mrs. Hannah Meerloo, long-time
resident of Carleton and noted philanthropist, was pronounced dead on arrival at Anglesworth Hospital early yesterday morning, following a fall down the cellar stairs in
her home on Tuttle Road. Mrs. Meerloo was
the widow of Jason Meerloo, killed in World
War II, and had lived in Carleton since 1953.

In the house at the time of the accident
were her niece, Leonora Harrington, who

had arrived just that day for a visit; a house guest, Hubert Holton, and her summer chauffeur, John Tuttle, a graduate student of Union College. Of the accident Miss Harrington said, "I heard this terrible scream and when I turned on my bedside light it was five minutes after one in the morning. I raced into the hall and bumped into Mr. Holton, who'd heard it, too. We knocked on my aunt Hannah's door and then went in and found her lights burning but the room empty. We began searching for her, not knowing where the scream came from, and then we heard a pounding on the kitchen door.

"It was Aunt Hannah's chauffeur, Jay, who sleeps over the garage adjoining the house. He'd heard the scream too. We finally found her lying at the foot of the cellar stairs. She must have been going down to the safe—there were canceled checks lying all around her. She was always up late nights, and the safe is in the basement, in the old preserve closet."

Miss Harrington was admitted to hospital suffering from shock and gave this account this morning upon being discharged.

Joe said in an astonished voice, "It's real then, Amelia: a very odd and disputable death."

We were silent then, each of us immersed, I think, in this explosion of theory meeting fact. Hannah had written that she believed she was going to be murdered, and here was Hannah's death described for us: a bizarre accident in the middle of the night, one of those inexplicable tragedies that *do* happen to people occasionally, except that more than a decade later we possessed Hannah's note.

Joe said, puzzled, "But how was it done, considering what we know from her letter? And by whom? She *knew* these people, Amelia."

"I think a successful murder has to be like a magic trick," I said slowly. "Like sleight-of-hand, Joe, with something moving faster than the eye can follow."

He said, "Give me Hannah's note to read again."

I dug it out of my purse and while he reread her letter I finished scanning the rest of the news column. It was Hannah's obituary, but the pattern and shape of her life had begun to matter to me now as much as her death. It said:

Mrs. Meerloo was born Hannah Maria Gruble in Pittsfield, Mass., in 1925, the daughter of a carpenter and a schoolteacher. At 18 she married Jason Meerloo, whose father was an inventor who made millions from his various patents and inventions, a fortune his son Jason inherited several months before his tragic death in France. Left widowed and wealthy at an early age Mrs. Meerloo traveled extensively for several years and is believed to be the first American woman to have visited Tibet. In 1950, using her maiden name of Gruble she published a book for young people entitled "The Maze in the Heart of the Castle," of which the New York *Times* wrote, "a small classic, a book for adults as well as children, full of enchantment and insights." It is the only book Mrs. Meerloo is known to have written.

In 1953 she purchased the old Whitney house on Tuttle Road in Carleton and lived there in semi-seclusion with her housekeeper. She endowed and built the Greenacres Private Psychiatric Hospital near Portland, established in 1946 the Jason Meerloo Orphanage in Anglesworth, and gave to this city the building which now houses the public library.

She leaves as survivors her niece, Leonora Harrington, of Boston, and a nephew, Robert Gruble, of New York City, professionally known as Robert Lamandale. Funeral plans are as yet incomplete.

A formal inquest into the death will be held on Thursday.

"Joe," I said, pointing to the last sentence.

"Inquest," he echoed. "Thank God! Find the inquest edition."

In a fury of haste I turned the pages of the August 5 edition. This time it was on the second page of the newspaper and Nora's age was listed as twenty-four; Hubert Holton, forty, was described as an associate professor of Political Science at Maine's Union College; John Tuttle was introduced as a graduate student, age twenty-seven, who had chauffeured summers for Mrs. Meerloo for nine years.

"That's a very respectable group," I said, taken aback.

"What did you expect, the Mafia?" countered Joe.

It was not a long report. Dr. Timothy Cox gave his testimony: death due to a basal skull fracture, with subdural bleeding. When asked to enlarge upon this he explained it as bleeding between the pia matter and arachnoid, a wound, he said, that fitted with the circumstances of her death, in this case the head striking cement, causing instant unconsciousness. She had been

104

unconscious but still alive—barely, he said—when he reached the house. She had died in the ambulance.

Nora repeated the story that had been given earlier to the newspaper, and both the chauffeur and the house guest confirmed that they had been awakened by a scream in the middle of the night. The only new person to give testimony was the housekeeper, a Mrs. Jane Morneau, age forty-two, who said it was customary for Mrs. Meerloo to give her, and any other help, their vacations during the month of July because July was "when Mr. Robin or Miss Nora, or both, came to visit her." Mrs. Morneau said that on July first, the day she left for her holiday, Miss Harrington had already been there, "and very high-spirited she was," and had been there for a week. She recalled vague plans for Miss Harrington and Mrs. Meerloo to be driven to New York City by John Tuttle to see Mr. Robin in a new play he was appearing in on Broadway. Mr. Holton's name was vaguely familiar to her but she was sure he was no friend of Mrs. Meerloo's. He had never come to the house before, and he was a stranger to her now.

The verdict by Judge Henry Tate was rendered as death by accident due to lack of evidence to the contrary.

Joe closed the volume thoughtfully. "Due to lack of evidence to the contrary," he repeated.

"Funny thing to insert," I said. "Don't they usually just say 'death by accident'?"

"I don't know," Joe said, frowning. "What strikes me first is, who is this Hubert Holton the housekeeper may have heard mentioned but had never seen before? Was he a friend of Nora's?"

"Yes, but there's something else, too," I pointed out, reaching for my spiral notebook. "Why did the first report in the newspaper say that Nora had 'just arrived for a visit' on the day of Hannah's death when the housekeeper testified she was already there on July first? Where had she been?"

Joe, still scowling, was lost in thought. I opened the notebook and wrote, *Hubert Holton,* underscored, and then, *If Nora was away, for how long was she gone?* I wrote down the other names given, too: Judge Henry Tate, Dr. Timothy Cox, Mrs. Jane Morneau.

"Three people," Joe said abruptly, with a shake of his head. "Just three people in the house at the time, aside from Hannah, of course: Nora and this Holton chap and the chauffeur John Tuttle in the adjoining building. But Hannah writes about 'the faceless ones.' Who could *they* have been? Do you suppose she could have been hallucinating?"

"Has it occurred to you," I said, "that her captors might have worn stocking masks when they brought her food? That could explain their facelessness."

"But what captors?" argued Joe. "The people in the house were known to her, Amelia. Even in stocking masks she would have recognized them: by their gestures, their walk, their voices."

"There could have been others in the house," I pointed out. "Nora was the only one related to her, and according to the newspaper account she had only just 'come back.' While she was gone there could have been others there, Joe. We have to find out how long Nora was away."

He nodded. "Okay, where do you suggest we start?"

"Why not at the very beginning?" I asked.

"Why not?" he grinned, and kissed me. "Let's go."

I replaced the volume of 1965 *Tribunes* and followed Joe up the stairs. But at the top I turned and looked back, knowing that I would never forget that electric, almost overpowering moment when I discovered that Hannah Meerloo was H. M. Gruble. Then Joe switched off the basement light and I followed him out to re-sume—or to really begin—our hunt for clues to a long-ago murder.

8

The real estate agent was a nice little man with a pink cherubic face and bright blue eyes. His name was Bob Tuttle—lots of Tuttles in Anglesworth, he said—and he drove us back to Carleton in his ancient Chevvy, pock-marked and stained from winter road salt.

We hadn't taken the time to visit the house yesterday, having become so very happily distracted, and so this was our first look at it. At first glance it was disappointing; I guess I'd expected a huge brick mansion after reading the word philanthropist in the local paper. It was large—ten rooms, Mr. Tuttle said—but it was just a comfortable, old-fashioned frame house with a porch running all around it and the south corner of the porch glassed in. It was an inconspicuous dun color that blended with the overgrown, frost-killed lawn around it, although on closer inspection it proved to have started out as olive-green.

"Needs a fresh paint job," Mr. Tuttle said cheerfully. "The Keppels had it only two years."

"How many people have owned it in the last, say, fifteen years?"

"Oh, a number," he said breezily. "Nice old house, you know, but then people see something small and modern and off they go."

Joe, following my line of thought, smiled. "Has it the reputation of being haunted maybe?"

Mr. Tuttle looked shocked as he braked beside the front steps of the house. "Lot of nonsense," he said indignantly. "We've long winters here and people like their gossip. You get just one person saying a thing like that and soon it's gospel truth. You can't believe everything you hear."

"I never do," I said innocently as he brought out a huge circle of keys with tags hanging from them. "Although as a matter of fact Joe and I adore haunted houses."

"Do you now," he said warily, and, having separated a group of keys from the others, he opened the car. door and climbed out. The three of us stood a moment on the circular graveled drive, a copse of birch trees to the right, a long flow of lawn on the left. The sun was shining and there were all kinds of delicious earth smells; spring was late up here but it was on its way, no doubt about it. Through the trees on the right I caught a glimpse of river flowing below the house.

We walked up wooden steps, crossed a wooden porch that crackled dryly under our feet, and entered a very cold house to begin a tour of its rooms.

Every house has its own personality but this one

was curiously neutral. Too many people in too few years, I guessed, but the wainscoting in the dining room was freshly painted and the kitchen was modern except for a very old wood-burning cookstove in one corner. *That* would have been Hannah's, I decided. There were fireplaces everywhere: in the long living room, in the dining room, in the kitchen, and one upstairs in the master bedroom, Mr. Tuttle said, but Joe announced that he'd like to see the basement first. "To have a look at the foundation and the sills," he said firmly. This earned him a look of such respect from Mr. Tuttle that from then on he addressed all of his remarks to Joe and ignored me.

The door to the cellar opened at the end of a very long hallway, which I found interesting. It was a hallway that began at the front door and ended at the cellar door, where one turned sharply right into the sunny kitchen behind the dining room. Set into this long hall were closets and a dumb-waiter. Mr. Tuttle turned on lights as we walked, and when he turned on the light to the cellar I was startled to find the stairs built of wood, not cement; somehow I had expected cement. These steps marched down at a moderately steep angle, but there was a handrail and nothing unusually dangerous except for the cement floor waiting at the bottom. I followed Joe and Mr. Tuttle down, feeling a little queasy, and stopped at the last step, staring at the floor where Hannah had been found lying unconscious. Of course there was nothing there. I turned and looked back up the stairs. The accepted story, as I understood it, was that Hannah had been carrying a handful of checks, had turned on the light, started down the stairs, lost her balance and fallen to the bottom. But there was something missing here, I thought, and the word was trajectory. The stairs were narrow and they were as steep as the usual basement staircase, laid out to conserve space, but still. . . .

"But still," I thought, "how could a body fall down wooden steps and be killed unless she was moving at some terrific speed when she approached the cellar stairs, or was hurled down?"

I was thinking even then of that long approach to the basement door, the hallway running almost the length of the house.

While Joe and Mr. Tuttle examined beams I went up and descended the stairs again, trying to imagine falling from this step or that one. If I lost my balance near the top, I thought, or from anywhere on the stairs, I would automatically throw out my hands to protect myself, wouldn't I? I'd stumble, bump against a step or two, grope for the handrail, hit a few stairs and possibly break an arm or a shoulder bone when I hit the cement but I couldn't understand anyone's being killed by the fall unless by some unimaginable fluke. I tried it again, climbing the stairs and this time closing the cellar door behind me, approaching it from the hall, reopening the door, pretending to turn on the light and then descending. Stopping for all these things made it even more impossible, unless a person were pushed. Or hurried down the hall blindfolded? Or dead before they went down?

"Let's go upstairs please," I said in a sudden, panicky voice. "Please. Now?"

Joe shot me a glance that included the stairs and up we went.

"This railing," I asked as we ascended. "Is it new?"

Bob Tuttle shook his head. "Old as the house and still sound," he said, tugging at it. "They knew how to build in those days. Mahogany, I'd guess."

A sound old railing, too. Why hadn't the doctor wondered about the trajectory and that sort of thing?

The staircase we mounted to the second floor curved in a lovely line. We inspected four bedrooms and two baths with interest before we moved on to the door of the attic. Here the arrangement was curious: the door opened on five shallow stairs and a landing, at which point the stairs turned abruptly right to continue up to the attic. At this landing there was a door.

"What's that?" I asked, pointing.

"What they used to call a box room," said Mr. Tuttle.

I let him lead us on up the stairs to the attic, where we found two maids' rooms, a lavatory, and walk-in closet smelling of mothballs, but I knew I wanted to see the box room.

"It's locked," said Mr. Tuttle.

"Just give me the key then," I told him, holding out my hand. "While you and Joe discuss price," I added brightly to make it worth his while, "because we plan a very *large* family. I have to see all the rooms."

After he'd gone through all his keys again I left them, and as soon as I unlocked and opened the door of the box room I *knew;* I knew in my bones and with every cell in my being that this was where Hannah had been held prisoner. In the first place it was the only room in the house without a window: there was just a metal vent high up near the ceiling with a tiny fan set into it. A solitary light bulb hung from the ceiling without a shade, and there was a rusty iron cot along one slanting wall that looked as if it had been there forever. The room measured roughly 12 by 14 except that the slanted ceiling made it look even smaller. It was empty except for the cot and an old bureau tilted on one leg that nobody had cared about enough to remove. The walls were plaster and had been painted not too long ago.

I sat down on the iron cot and looked around me at what Hannah would have seen, because I was *sure* now. A box room would have been where they stored trunks in Victorian days; there would have been one or two of those, I guessed, plus the hurdy-gurdy, and perhaps a few other pieces, possibly a rocking horse kept for Robin and Nora to play with when they were young. One of the trunks would have been filled with costumes—what made me know this?—for dressing-up fun on a rainy day. But I didn't think it would be a good place in which to be trapped: there would have been no daylight, and the mattress—if it was the same one— was filthy and full of lumps and holes. At times the room must have been stifling—it had been July, after all—and it must always have been claustrophobic.

I sat there and I said softly, "Hannah?" and then, "Hannah Gruble?"

I've never believed in ghosts, although I do believe that we leave something of ourselves behind us, some imprint of personality or essence, in all the places we live. I believe that people also affect us in this way by their vibrations. This is my only explanation for what happened to me after I spoke Hannah's name. I mean, if I didn't explain it in this way I would have to believe in ghosts, wouldn't I? But a sense of peace, of absolute calm—such as I'd experienced only in the presence of Amman Singh—flowed through me and transfixed me as I sat there. It was a feeling of unbelievable tranquility, almost of communion with someone, and it lasted until I heard Joe and Mr. Tuttle descending the stairs from the attic.

The sound of their footsteps brought me back to the moment with a start, and I remembered why I was here. Wondering if Hannah might have attempted any other messages I walked over to the bureau and examined it but the drawers were empty except for two

113

dead flies and something stuck to the top of one drawer. I had just pried it loose when Joe and Mr. Tuttle walked in.

"Nice house, don't you think, Joe?" I said. Glancing down into my hand I discovered that all I'd unearthed was a petrified wad of chewing gum.

Joe looked around with interest, lifted an eyebrow and nodded. "But it's four o'clock already, Amelia, I think we'd better go back to town and talk about it. Mr. Tuttle feels the owners are ready to come down in price quite a bit. It's all very tempting."

"Yes, isn't it?" I said eagerly. "Put a window in here and it would make a lovely little sewing room."

We moved out into the hall and I noticed that Bob Tuttle forgot to lock the box room. Joe was saying deliberately, "Mr. Tuttle tells me that Dr. Cox is dead but your mother's old friend Jane Morneau still lives in Anglesworth."

"Wonderful!" I exclaimed—we were turning into a regular vaudeville team, Joe and I—and remarking on the coincidences of life, of which the most amazing one Mr. Tuttle would never know, we walked out on the landing, down the several stairs to the second-floor hallway, followed it to the staircase, and thus left Hannah's house behind us.

Parting with Mr. Tuttle, however, proved less easy. He wanted to give us a good many judicious suggestions about the house, he wanted to counsel us on a possible price offer and to explain the attitude of the Keppels, while we in turn wanted to inquire about Hannah's will before the courthouse closed. It made for a tight squeak; in fact, it was precisely four-fifty when we raced up the stairs of the courthouse again. We ran down long hallways following signs of a flat yellow hand, with index finger pointing and the word PROBATE under them, until we reached a room that was high-ceilinged and cool, with a long counter and desks behind it, and walls lined with legal volumes. I was glad to stop running and catch my breath.

Joe asked the young woman who approached us if we might see the will of Hannah Meerloo, who had died on July 25, 1965. I had the terrible feeling that the clerk would say we needed a court order to see someone's will but she nodded in a matter-of-fact way, asked us to write the name on a piece of paper for her, and then disappeared into an adjoining room where I could see row upon row of records in drawers and on shelves. I looked at Joe and saw that he was fighting down his suspense. Presently the young woman returned and placed before us a single-page document with a signature at the bottom.

"You've just time to photostat it if you'd like," she said politely. "We close in two minutes. There's a machine behind you."

"Yes," I said, incredulous at its being so easy. "Yes, thank you."

We made two copies, handed back the original and hurried out of the building in a stream of departing clerks. We began our reading of the will seated outside on the steps in the fading sunshine.

"Joe, look at the date," I gasped. "July 2, 1965, only twenty-three days before she was killed."

"I'm looking," he said grimly.

The single sheet was neatly typed, with the signatures of three witnesses at the bottom. I read:

> Let it be known that this is the last Will and
> Testament of Hannah Gruble Meerloo, and
> that being of sound mind and body I, Hannah
> Gruble Meerloo, appoint as co-executors of
> my estate my nephew Robert Gruble of New

York, and my attorney Garwin Mason of Anglesworth.

Since the Greenacres Private Psychiatric Hospital has already been endowed by me with a permanent Trust Fund, and other charities of mine are now self-sustaining I bequeath to my loyal housekeeper Jane Whitney Morneau the sum of $35,000. and, renouncing all previous wills, ask that the remainder of my estate, once taxes have been removed, be divided equally in three ways: one-third of the residual to my niece Leonora Harrington of Boston, one-third to my nephew Robert Gruble of New York, and one-third to my protégé John Tuttle of Carleton, with the hope that he may see fit to continue contributions when necessary to the support of the Jason Meerloo Orphanage in Anglesworth, in which he spent his early years.

Signed on this 2nd day of July 1965,
Hannah Gruble Meerloo
witnessed by:
  Daniel Lipton
  Hubert Holton
  Leonora Harrington

We finished reading at the same time. Joe said, "John Tuttle's the name of the young man who was driving for her summers."

"Enter chauffeur," I said, nodding. "Enter a witness named Daniel Lipton. Re-enter Hubert Holton."

"And Nora witnessed the will, too," mused Joe.

"I see that," I said, and I stared down at this innocent sheet of paper, wishing I could shake it until its secrets tumbled out. "Joe, I think we've got to see this man Garwin Mason next, don't you? Hannah's attorney, I mean, to see what he says about this will. If he's still alive," I added.

"Let's find out," said Joe.

We drove two blocks to a public phone booth where I found Garwin Mason's name listed in the directory under Mason, Gerard and Tuttle. It was after five o'clock but I telephoned anyway, and was surprised to hear a live secretary answer. I asked if we might see Mr. Garwin Mason. The secretary said that he'd already left, and she was just leaving, that Mr. Mason had to be in court the next morning at ten o'clock but that I could see him before then at half-past eight. I made the appointment, gave her my name, and hung up.

It was now half-past five. I looked up Jane Morneau in the directory and found that she lived at 23 Farnsworth Road; I put in a call to her too but there was no answer and so Joe and I decided to have dinner next which, considering that we'd had no lunch, seemed a reasonable thing to do.

"And what do we use as bait for Mr. Garwin Mason at half-past eight tomorrow morning?" asked Joe pleasantly.

We were seated in the coffee shop of the Golden Kingfisher Motel, where thirty minutes earlier we had checked into unit 18. We each had a seafood platter in front of us, a milk shake, and a copy of Hannah's will.

"I think," I said firmly, having already considered this, "that I should visit him alone and tell him I'm writing a biography of Hannah Gruble, author."

Joe grinned. "Your inventiveness astounds me, Miss Jones."

117

"It does me, too," I admitted, "but in a sense it *is* like research for a biography, Joe, so it's not an outright lie. Lawyers don't thaw easily."

"You make him sound like a frozen steak."

"Well," I said vaguely, "there's client confidentiality and all that, isn't there? Joe, this will has to be the paper Hannah was forced to sign before she died, don't you think?"

"The date's wrong," he pointed out. "The will was drawn up the second and she died the twenty-fifth. We can't suppose otherwise until you've seen Mr. Mason tomorrow, because if *he* drew up that will for Hannah—"

"I don't for a moment believe that he did," I told him flatly. "She wrote in her note that whatever she signed the night before was her death warrant. I can't think of anything else a person would sign that could be so damning."

"Okay," said Joe, relenting, "suppose Garwin Mason *didn't* draw up the will for her and it's a phony, or was drawn up by the people who killed her. Remember Hannah's note? She'd signed whatever it was the night before she was killed, and she was killed the twenty-fifth."

"It could have been typed up the twenty-second or twenty-third of July but dated earlier to avert suspicion."

Joe said patiently, "But Nora's signature is on it, and Nora wasn't in Carleton until a few hours before Hannah's death. She'd just 'come back,' remember?"

"Damn," I said, and thought about this. "Then suppose somebody typed up the will on July 2, using Hannah's typewriter to be certain just in case, persuaded the witnesses to sign it, and sometime after that Hannah was locked into the box room until she herself signed it."

118

"That sounds better."

"Oh Joe."

"Steady there."

"Yes, but think of the kind of mind that could conceive of this," I said, tears rising to my eyes. "To take an unprotected woman and lock her up in a room *in her own home,* Joe, until her spirit is crushed—and the worst of it, people coming to the house, tradesmen, neighbors perhaps, and never suspecting. The cold-blooded ruthlessness of it, Joe!"

He nodded. "All the more important we find who did it, Amelia."

I glanced down at the will in front of me. "We have to find out what's different in this will from any other wills she made. Do you think Garwin Mason will tell me? I can already hazard a guess."

Joe, reading my mind, shook his head. "You have to keep your mind open in this sort of thing, Amelia, not leap to conclusions or let preconceived ideas spring up too early."

"Of course," I said politely, "except I do think it's very odd, her leaving one third to this John Tuttle, who's not related at all."

He grinned. "Okay, so why don't you look in the directory and see if there's still a Jason Meerloo Orphanage here in Anglesworth?"

"I already did," I told him quietly. "After I called Mr. Mason's office and before I looked up Mrs. Morneau's number. Which reminds me that I'd better try her number again."

"Great," said Joe dryly as I got up, "and was there, or was there not, an orphanage listed?"

"No orphanage," I told him. "John Tuttle did *not* keep it afloat as she hoped in her will."

Joe looked at me with an odd smile on his lips. "But

Amelia, aren't you forgetting that if our suppositions are correct *Hannah didn't write that will?*"

I dropped back into my chair again, neatly floored by this jab. I said helplessly, "But that makes it a *very* strange will, Joe. I can't belive Nora's involved, she must have loved her aunt—"

"But her signature's on the will," Joe reminded me.

"I'm betting it was forged or gotten under false pretenses, but if she *was* involved," I pointed out, "that makes it even stranger because she cut herself off from one third of a lot of money And if John Tuttle was involved he tied himself to supporting an orphanage with his money. Quite publicly, too."

"Wait—be patient," said Joe. "Tomorrow we make absolutely certain that Hannah's attorney did *not* draw up this will. We verify."

"That word again," I said indignantly, and left him and went to the telephone. I dropped a dime in the slot, dialed Mrs. Morneau's number, and after listening to it ring and ring I replaced the receiver. I dug out my spiral notebook and consulted names again and then looked up Daniel Lipton in the directory. There was no Daniel listed but there was a Mrs. Daniel Lipton living at 13½ Pearl Street. I copied the address, stopped at the counter to buy a map of Anglesworth on display there, and went back to the table to tell Joe.

"Okay," he said after a glance at his watch. "I suggest we wrap up this bacchanalian feast with a couple of hot fudge sundaes and then go and see if she's related, but first I'll call my answering service and tell them where I am."

Joe took his turn at telephoning and when he came back he looked pleased. "Ken says it looks as if the hearing's been postponed again, so we can relax."

"Beautiful," I said, and felt ten pounds lighter despite the enormous sundae on which I was gorging.

Pearl Street was a forgotten dirt road behind a supermarket and a movie house, obviously one of the last stops in Anglesworth on the road down. There were only six houses on the street, but any differences in their architecture had long ago been erased by the erosions of apathy: broken windows stuffed with blankets, sagging porches, peeling paint and loose garbage spilling out of rusting pails and cardboard cartons. When we drew up to number 13½ a rat slunk away from a plastic pail and gave us a sullen look over his shoulder. By the time we reached the front door of 13½ he was back again; I noticed a sizable number of empty wine and gin bottles among the refuse.

The bell wasn't working; we knocked and then called, and after an interval a woman opened the door and said suspiciously, "Yeah?"

"Mrs. Lipton?" asked Joe. "Mrs. Daniel Lipton?"

She peered at us blurredly. Her face was a circle of desiccated flesh with heavy pouches under her eyes and chin. She was wearing a long flowered cotton skirt, a moth-eaten gray cardigan, a green sweater under that, and a black turtleneck under *that*. She was all layers, it was hard to define a figure behind them. Her hair was a frizzy blond with gray showing at the roots and there was a thick smear of crimson covering her mouth. "Good or bad?" she asked in a hoarse whiskey voice, and looked over Joe admiringly. "Good news, okay. Bad, come tomorrow."

"We're trying to trace a Mr. Daniel Lipton," Joe told her. "Around 1965 he had some connection with Mrs. Hannah Meerloo, and witnessed a will she made in July of that year."

121

"Danny?" she said and shrugged. "If you got the price of a bottle I'll let you in."

Joe took out a five-dollar bill and she grabbed it. "Tom?" she called over her shoulder and opened the door wider to let us in.

We walked into a cold hallway and then into a dark living room. The reason it was so dark was that venetian blinds had been drawn over each of the two windows, and the only light came from the television tube, which glowed eerily and across which a wagon train was riding at full gallop. Silhouetted against this ghostly illumination sat three men, stiffly upright. I thought at first they might be dead and propped up in their chairs, they sat so still and straight, not even turning at our arrival, but one of them slowly stirred, detached himself, and walked over to Mrs. Lipton. Wordlessly she gave him the five-dollar bill and without any change of expression he glided out of the house, closing the door behind him.

Mrs. Lipton led us to a couch with broken springs in the back of the room and we sat down. "So?" she said, staring at us.

"You're related to the Daniel Lipton who knew Mrs. Meerloo and witnessed her last will in 1965?"

She moved her eyes from us to the wall, apparently to think about this. "He did yard-work for her sometimes. Not regular-like but when she needed extra help. The big house in Carleton?"

"Yes."

She nodded. "Yep, that's Danny." She gave a cackle. "Landscape gardening's what it said on his truck. Most of it, between you'n me, was grass-cutting. But that was a long time ago. Any money in this for me?" she asked, suddenly staring at us again.

"He was your husband?" I asked.

"Well," she began, and sniffed, brought a tattered

Kleenex from her pocket and blew her nose, "he *was*." She thought about this, too, her head tilted; appeared to reach some conclusion, opened her mouth to speak, and then sighed and closed it. "Bastard," she said finally, in a sentimental voice. "He could put it away faster'n anybody I met since."

"Since what?" asked Joe quickly.

"Since he got—" Whatever it was I didn't hear because the Indians began attacking the wagon train on the television screen and the room was suddenly filled with war whoops.

Joe was sitting closer to her. "You mean he's dead?" I heard him say.

"Dead!" Her shriek filled the room, louder than the howling Indians. "Hey boys," she shouted, "this guy wants to know if Danny's dead."

I thought I heard polite titters, but neither of the remaining two heads turned. She said to Joe, "A long time ago, buster, and it ain't been easy for me since."

I could bet it hadn't; I wondered how many bottles lay between then and now. "*How* long?" I asked, pursuing this picture of enough empty bottles to reach Chicago or possibly Denver.

"Nineteen sixty-five it was," she said. "Christmas Eve when they told me."

The front door opened and Tom glided back into the room carrying a heavy paper bag; from the weight of it there must have been two or three bottles inside. Mrs. Lipton sprang to her feet, pulled out one of the bottles, wrung it open, took a long drink, shivered, and handed it to Tom. "Party night," she giggled.

"Mrs. Lipton," Joe said, and then louder, "Mrs. Lipton—"

She looked at us in surprise. "You still here? I got no more to say. He's dead."

We got up from the couch but Joe had apparently

heard her words better than I during the Indian on-slaught because he shouted at her, "You said he was *killed*, Mrs. Lipton?"

"Did I?" she said, surprised. "Well, he's dead, that's for sure, and there's the door." Just to be sure we found it she walked over, opened it and held it for us.

We were already on the porch when she shouted after us angrily, "Got his throat slit from ear to ear down by the river Christmas Eve, that's what, and they never learnt who did it or tried very hard neither, the bastards."

When we spun around to look at her the door was shut.

Christmas Eve 1965, I thought. Five months after Hannah's death, almost to the day.

We walked to the van and climbed in. It was dusk now but the dimming of light didn't improve the view any. I said quietly, "Let's get out of here, Joe."

Joe made no move to start the van. He said grimly, "Amelia—"

"What?"

"It's not too late, you know. This happened a long time ago, and life has—well, arranged itself around it now. Adjusted itself."

So it was Joe who was feeling scared now; on the other hand I was beginning to glimpse patterns and whorls, all of them horrible but nevertheless taking on vague shapes behind the nearly impenetrable fog. "I don't think life has arranged itself around this death very happily," I pointed out. "And we're just beginning to get somewhere," I reminded him.

"Yes, but where, Amelia?"

"Closer to a murder."

"*And* a murderer," he pointed out. "A murderer who got away with violence a long time ago, Amelia."

I said, "You're thinking what I am, then? That Daniel Lipton may have been murdered because of something he knew about Hannah's death?"

"And before he could talk," Joe said, starting the van at last and shifting into gear. "After all, if he drank like his wife—he witnessed that will, Amelia, and everything points now to its being a bogus will."

"Still to be verified," I reminded him with a smile, but I considered his words thoughtfully as we bumped over the potholes and left Pearl Street behind. I wondered why they left me unmoved. Since morning, when I'd learned that Hannah was H. M. Gruble all my doubts seemed to have vanished. I remembered Amman Singh saying to me once that the important events of our lives are already laid out for us in a pattern that we can't see or understand, and that these events are inescapable. I'd always supposed that I would follow this wherever it took me but now I felt that it was inevitable, as if it had been waiting for me all along.

Of course I was forgetting that until recently my hold on life had been very light, very tenuous, and that my judgment might be askew. I forgot that I was still convalescent—comparatively unlived, so to speak— and that Joe might be seeing more clearly than I. But when accosted with decisions—which are frankly hell for me to make—my motto is always "consider the alternative," and I just couldn't conceive of what my life would be like if I walked away from this. I no longer had choice; I was already inside of it, I had passed the point of no return.

"I can't back out, Joe," I told him flatly. "Even if you do, I can't now."

He said darkly, "I thought I'd fall in love with some nice wholesome all-American girl whose idea of a good time was doing crossword puzzles and admiring me."

"Isn't life amazing?" I said cheerfully, and we climbed the steps to unit 18, unlocked the door, walked inside, and bolted it behind us.

9

At twenty-five minutes past eight the next morning I left Joe curled up in the van again with *Astronomy for the Layman*—he was certainly having trouble making headway in it—and walked into the offices of Mason, Gerard and Tuttle. There was a nice waiting room, white walls with seascapes that hadn't been reproduced by an office supply house but selected with care and expense from art shows: one was an original Marin. When I told the secretary who I was, she said I was expected and pointed to one of the four doors opening on to the waiting room. I walked into an office that was wall-to-wall books, except for one space over Mr.

Mason's desk in which there hung a really fine Buffet print of a sailboat with the wind lifting its sails.

Mr. Mason glanced up at my entrance, and then rose to shake hands. He looked far beyond retirement age, eighty at least, but there was nothing frail about him: his face was weatherbeaten, he was bald except for a thatch of white hair encircling his skull and his eyes were an unbleached vivid blue, narrowed now in their appraisal of me. I had the feeling that I was being weighed, measured and dissected with uncanny penetration and I felt sorry for anyone who faced him with a guilty conscience. Yet I liked him at once; he was, to use a very old-fashioned word, a gentleman. He had presence. It was obvious in the soft, courteous voice that suggested I sit down, Miss Jones, and in the way he remained standing until I did so; in the reserved but kindly smile that put me at ease and the courtly manner in which he asked what he could do for me.

"I'm writing a biography of Hannah Gruble," I said firmly. "Or Mrs. Meerloo, of course, and in my research I've come to the facts of her death." I placed the Xeroxed copy of her will on his desk, and added, "Your name is mentioned in the will, and so it occurred to me . . . that is, there are a few questions left unanswered about her death."

"And in what way can I be of help, Miss Jones?" he asked. He reached for a pair of glasses, put them on, glanced at the will, removed his glasses and restored his gaze to me.

I said innocently, "This will was, of course, drawn up by you personally?"

There was an edge to his voice when he said, "No, it was *not*."

"I see," I said, my heart beating faster at this acknowledgement. "But surely where it mentions you as

127

her attorney, and you were appointed co-executor of the will—"

He interrupted me. "The will was not written in this office, Miss Jones. I can assure you that as a graduate of the Harvard Law School no will constructed in my office would read as this one does."

I said with all the ingenuousness I could summon, "You've written other wills for her, of course."

He gave me a sharp glance. "Yes."

"You had been her attorney then for many years?"

His voice was dry. "Yes, Miss Jones."

"May I ask why she didn't have you write this one for her, sir? I mean, were you away, perhaps, on—" I took a moment to examine the date, as if I didn't already know it by heart. "On July 2, 1965?"

"No, Miss Jones, I was in my office. Just as I am today."

"Then didn't you—er—wonder, sir, at her not contacting you? You must surely have felt rather—well, surprised?"

"Is this a court of law, Miss Jones?" he inquired with humor.

I looked at him, and I realized that something had changed in the atmosphere since I'd begun asking my questions, but where I would have supposed there would be tension—a reaction of anger or disapproval— it was quite the opposite: Mr. Mason had relaxed. He was wary but he was relaxed and waiting. But waiting for what, I wondered.

So I went at once to the point. "Mr. Mason," I said, meeting his eyes directly, "I would like very much to know—I realize it's confidential information but I would like to ask—and after all, so much time has elapsed and your client is dead—"

"Yes, Miss Jones?" he asked.

I took a deep breath. "I would like to ask how this

will differs from previous wills you drew up for her in your office."

"Ah . . ." It was like a sigh, a long expelling of breath that seemed to fill and haunt the room before it reached an end. He sat looking at me, and those ancient eyes—still so blue—seemed to go through and through me. He said, "It *is* confidential information you're asking for, Miss Jones, you are quite correct in that."

"Yes," I said.

"You seem an oddly determined young woman," he added with a twisted little smile. "You are not from these parts, Miss Jones?"

"From Trafton, Pennsylvania."

He nodded. "This is a curious corner of Maine, Miss Jones. I have lived here for over fifty years and yet I am still an outsider. They will say of me that I'm 'from away.' Hannah, too, was 'from away.' We live here surrounded by Liptons, Tuttles, Pritchetts, and Gerards."

"You called her Hannah," I said eagerly.

He did not reply to this. He was silent for a moment and then he said, "Her previous wills were very similar to each other but not similar to this will of July 2, 1965, Miss Jones, no. Over the years that she lived here—first in Anglesworth, in the house she later donated to the town for a library, and then in Carleton—she made perhaps half a dozen wills, changing them to fit circumstances but only in minor ways. In all of them she left a stated amount to her housekeeper, Jane Morneau, and she bequeathed sums to the Greenacres Psychiatric Hospital and to the Jason Meerloo Orphanage. The residual—and we are talking here of perhaps two million dollars after taxes—"

"Two million!" I exclaimed.

"—was to be divided between her nephew Robin and her niece Nora."

"But there was never before any mention of—" I

stopped abruptly. "I appreciate your giving me this—this confidential information, sir."

He bowed courteously, mockingly. "But then as you have pointed out, Miss Jones, it happened many years ago and my client is dead. You have read her book, of course."

"Oh, yes," I said. "Many times, and I own a first edition."

He nodded. "A pity it's out of print. I've always felt that if the sequel could have been published it would have firmly established *The Maze in the Heart of the Castle* as the classic it deserves to be."

"Did she ever consider writing a sequel?" I asked.

"I believe that she had completed one at the time of her death."

"What?" I gasped. "Do you mean that? A second one, after so many years?" I was incredulous. "But what happened to it? It was never published, was it?"

"I doubt that many people knew of it," he told me with a shrug. "People were accustomed to her scribblings, as she called it, every morning. I know of it only because in her previous will—drawn up two months before this one—she specifically mentioned leaving her niece and nephew the right to apply for copyright renewals on *The Maze in the Heart of the Castle,* and—if it was published—a book entitled *In the Land of the Golden Warriors.* A sequel to the first, she called it."

I whistled faintly. "And the manuscript was never found? Nobody knew?" And then it hit me. "You say a previous will was drawn up *only two months* before the July 2 one?"

He nodded, watching me with interest.

"Mr. Mason," I said, "wasn't anyone—surely you must have been skeptical—just a little—of this final July will? Didn't it seem strange, the circumstances and all, at the time? Strange to someone?"

I had the strangest impression that I had met with his approval; his smile was that of an instructor with an apt pupil. "It seemed strange to one person, her nephew Robin," he said. "Robin insisted on a Probate Court hearing."

"A hearing," I repeated, not understanding.

He explained. "A will is filed in probate shortly after the death of the testatrix. Following this a legal notice called a citation is issued to all the heirs, listing the terms of the will, and if any heir objects or feels that his or her rights have been violated they may ask for a hearing in the Probate Court."

"I see," I said breathlessly. "So there was an investigation, or at least a hearing into all this? Would there be any records still available?"

"There are always records," he assured me. "Court stenographers take down each word in court, you know, and although officially the records belong to the court stenographer they can be purchased."

I sighed. "Oh dear, after so many years would there still be a copy?"

"I can lend you mine," he said with his curious little smile, and rang for his secretary. "I couldn't represent Robin because I was named co-executor of the estate but I followed the hearing closely and took pains to secure a copy for my files. My partner Mr. Gerard handled the case. Miss Edmonds," he said when she entered the room, "will you fetch us the probate hearings on the Hannah Meerloo will—October 1965, I believe. Late October."

"Yes, sir."

"And a large manila envelope so that this young lady can return the document to me by mail."

She was gone and we smiled at each other politely, but I was feeling uneasy by now. I felt as if I were no longer leading this conversation but was being tantalized in some obscure way, or subtly directed. There were a dozen questions I longed to ask him but I knew that the rules of the game were his, and his courtesy would extend only so far.

A moment later Miss Edmonds was back. Garwin Mason glanced over what looked to be a two-inch-thick sheaf of printed matter, nodded, tucked it into a large envelope, and handed it across the desk to me. "There you are, Miss Jones," he said. "Just return this, it's all I ask."

"I will," I promised and stood up to go. "And thank you."

I had reached the door when he said, "Miss Jones." I stopped and turned.

He was polishing his reading glasses with an immaculate white handkerchief but now he paused and looked at me, and although his face was stern his eyes were kind. "You are not writing a biography of Hannah Gruble." It was a statement, not a question.

"No, sir."

He nodded. "I didn't, for more than one or two moments, assume so."

"Then you've been very patient with me, sir."

He said dryly, "No, Miss Jones, grateful. For years I've lived with the mystery of Hannah Meerloo's last will and I can now exchange that mystery for another: why a young woman scarcely out of her teens has suddenly begun asking the questions about Hannah's will that were never properly answered in 1965."

"Questions *were* asked, then, in 1965?" I asked curiously.

"A few," he said. "But as I also mentioned, we are surrounded here, Miss Jones, by Pritchetts and Tuttles, Liptons and Gerards. The questions were only—unfortunately—tolerated."

"Mr. Mason," I said impulsively, "what was she like?"

"Hannah?" He looked at me and then his gaze moved to the corner of the room, and probably into the past as well. He said thoughtfully, "I always find it difficult to describe her, Miss Jones. I could tell you that she had dark hair, gray eyes, small regular features, nothing distinguishing about either them or her. I think in 1965 she would have been called a plain-looking woman, although fashions in beauty change, as you may be too young to realize yet. Possibly she was even a woman you would have passed by on the street without a second glance—I've been told that she was—but I will say this," he added with a slight smile, "that ever since knowing her I have never ceased to give a second glance, even a third, to every plain woman I see on the street."

"Meaning what?" I asked, caught by something in his voice.

"Meaning that I am an old man, Miss Jones, nearing eighty. I have met a great many people in my lifetime and what has impressed me about the majority of them is the smallness of their souls. Pinched, shrunken, undernourished. Hannah Meerloo was in fact—literally—the most beautiful woman I have ever known."

"Beautiful," I whispered, nodding.

"She had an eager, childlike quality which, Miss Jones, if I may say so, I see somewhat repeated in yourself. But there was added to it a kind of magic: if you once spoke to her you never forgot her. She never lost a sense of wonder, she made one notice things. She was a woman who loved life."

"Loved life," I repeated, and then, very quietly, I said, "Thank you very much, Mr. Mason. Thank you *very* much."

"Amelia," Joe said when I joined him in the van, "you look funny again. You have these interviews and you come out of them looking the way people do when they've seen a Hitchcock or a Bergman film."

"It's possible," I said. "Joe, he knew her. She was a plain woman, he said, but the most beautiful he's ever known."

"That will take time to puzzle out," Joe said. "What about facts? And what's that enormous envelope you're carrying?"

"A copy of the court hearing that Robin asked for," I told him breathlessly, "and it should prove a heck of a lot more interesting to read than *Astronomy for the Layman,* Joe, because they only have probate hearings when an heir protests a will. And, Joe—Mr. Mason says Hannah had just finished writing a second book, *In the Land of the Golden Warriors*—and he did *not* draw up this will for her, he was in his office that day, July 2, but never contacted, and in all the other wills the residual or whatever it is was divided between only Robin and Nora. And Joe, he'd drawn up a will for Hannah only *two months before this one.*"

"We've hit paydirt again," Joe said, starting up the van.

"No," I said suddenly, "I think we've just entered the maze in the heart of the castle. Joe, where are you taking us?"

"Back to the motel to start reading," he said, and headed the van out into traffic.

We sat next each other on the bed in unit 18 with doughnuts and coffee on the table beside us. "Skip the preliminaries," Joe said as I removed the pages from their envelope. "Find the important parts and read them aloud."

"Mmmmm," I murmured, scanning the first page.

134

"Well, here we go," I said eagerly. "Robin is definitely accusing John Tuttle, boy chauffeur, of exercising undue influence on the testatrix, or Hannah."

"Hooray," Joe said, pulling out a pillow and punching it. "The plot thickens."

"Or sickens," I reminded him. "Robin points out that Hannah had drawn up that new will in April, carefully prepared by her attorney, Garwin Mason, but that this new will of July 2 was written without the knowledge of her lawyer, that two of its witnesses are unknown to him—this is Robin speaking—and that all previous wills made by his aunt were always discussed with him and Nora, and they were sent copies. *Copies,* Joe."

"Okay, go on. . . ."

"That the contents of the July 2 will were unknown to his cousin Nora when she signed as a witness—hmmm, that's interesting—and that this sudden inclusion of John Tuttle, his aunt's chauffeur—even though his aunt had a very real interest in his career and had financed his college education—has deprived him and his cousin Nora of their rightful, legal, and previously stipulated legacies."

"The lines are drawn," Joe said, nodding. "The operative word is now Undue Influence."

"Oboy, here we go," I said, reaching page four. "Hubert Holton testifies."

Joe slid flat on the bed and placed the pillow across his stomach. "Every word, Amelia. Every nuance."

"They don't provide nuances," I said crossly. "In fact it's just question and answer, with the names of the witness and lawyer at the top of the page. But here I go, it's Mr. Gerard questioning Mr. Holton."

Q. Mr. Holton, would you explain, please, how you came to be staying at Mrs. Hannah Meerloo's home during the month of July?

A. Certainly, sir. I was on vacation, tour-

135

ing Maine. Passing through Anglesworth I
thought I'd stop in or at least telephone Jay
Tuttle to say hello. John Tuttle, that is. John
was a student of mine at Union College—a
brilliant student—and I'd become very interested in his future, an interest, I might
add, that was obviously shared by Mrs.
Meerloo, who had seen his potential when
he was at the Orphanage she founded.

Q. But you had never met Mrs. Hannah
Meerloo before?

A. No, sir. I telephoned Jay—John Tuttle, that is—from Anglesworth on July second. He suggested my coming out to Carleton for an evening of talk, he explained that
he occupied the apartment over the garage
and how to find him. In turn I suggested my
arriving earlier than that and taking him
back to Anglesworth for dinner. I arrived at
his apartment about five o'clock, we had a
drink or two and before leaving for dinner
he wanted Mrs. Meerloo to meet me.

"Suspicious amount of detail there," interposed Joe.
"He sounds as if he's on trial for murder."

"Perhaps he thought he was," I said dryly, and continued.

A. After meeting Mrs. Meerloo she very
kindly insisted that I have dinner there with
her and Miss Harrington and Jay—John
Tuttle—who apparently dined regularly with
them. He was not the usual chauffeur, you
see, he drove for her summers as a way of
paying her back for her kindness.

Q. So you would say that summers Mr.

John Tuttle was more or less a member of the family?

A. Well, it all seemed very informal, and they were certainly on very friendly terms.

Q. Mrs. Meerloo then invited you to remain as a house guest?

A. I believe it was actually Nora's idea, sir. Miss Nora Harrington. We did have a particularly stimulating and interesting evening discussing books and politics—I teach political science—and Nora somewhat impulsively asked her aunt if I couldn't stay the weekend. They had a tennis court, you see, and I play tennis. Nora pointed out that with Robin not there she'd have a tennis partner and also she could show me the local sights.

Q. But you stayed longer than the weekend, Mr. Holton?

A. Yes. I was there until—until the tragic and most regrettable accident that happened on the twenty-fifth of July.

Q. Also at Nora's invitation?

A. I don't really recall, sir. I would mention leaving, and no one would hear of it, and frankly I was enjoying their company very much. It was much pleasanter than idle sightseeing and staying alone in motels.

Q. Mr. Holton, how would you describe John Tuttle's relationship with Mrs. Meerloo?

A. Oh, charming, absolutely charming. He obviously thought the world of Miss Hannah, as he called her.

Q. Would you describe any incident in which, in your estimation, John Tuttle might have exercised "undue influence" upon Mrs. Meerloo in changing her will to his benefit?

A. I must remind you, sir, that I was asked to sign the will as a witness that very first evening I came to see John and stayed over for dinner. That is to say, I have carefully checked my diary on this matter of dates. I arrived in Anglesworth the night of July 1 and phoned Jay—John, that is—on the morning of the second of July, which is the same day that I met Mrs. Meerloo for the first time. But I was after this a member of the household for three weeks—as house guest—and I frankly cannot imagine on what Mr. Robert Gruble bases this alleged undue influence unless—

Q. Unless what, Mr. Holton?

A. Unless it was the fact that the relationship between Jay Tuttle and Mrs. Meerloo was more like that of mother and son, and some jealousy might have been involved, but that is, of course, only speculation.

Q. Yes it is, Mr. Holton, and quite unsolicited and uncalled for. The court is interested only in facts, not speculation.

A. Yes, sir. Sorry, sir.

"Ha," intervened Joe, sitting up and leaning closer to look at the page. "He got that in very smoothly; neat little touch, what? Robin, the displaced son-nephew, jealous of the interloper, Charming Jay. Or John, that is, as Holton kept saying. Who testifies next?"

"Nora," I said, "and I don't understand the tennis business, or the drives, if Nora was going to leave soon afterward. Move a little, Joe, you're throwing a shadow across the page."

"Read on," he said, removing himself two inches.

"Okay, here's Nora: Leonora Hannah Harrington of Boston, daughter of Patience Gruble, Hannah's sister, questioned by Gerard."

> Q. Now, Miss Harrington . . . A statement was made by you to the newspapers that you had arrived at your aunt's house only a few hours before her tragic accident on July 25?
>
> A. Yes, sir.
>
> Q. Yet at the inquest it was stated by Mrs. Morneau, your aunt's housekeeper, that you arrived in June, a week early for your usual July visit with your aunt. You were not with your aunt then for the major part of July?
>
> A. Oh yes, I was there. I joined Aunt Hannah on June 26, and was with her until her accident, with the exception of two days when I drove to my apartment in Boston on July 23 for more clothes. You see, there was talk of us going to New York City late in July to see Robin in his new play, and I needed city clothes for that. Except—except of course we never drove to New York. . . . That awful night happened instead.

I read this statement and then I read it again. Of course I knew that Nora's signature was on the will but I'd given her the benefit of every doubt. To do anything else would have struck me as monstrous, inhuman. It still did. I couldn't believe it.

"I can't believe it," Joe said, voicing my own thought. "Nora was there—all through July—except for two days?"

"She couldn't have been so cruel," I said flatly. "Joe,

139

she couldn't have been in on it, there has to be an explanation."

"Like what?" asked Joe.

"They could have made her a prisoner, too. Or black-mailed her."

Joe took the transcript from me and read aloud the remainder of Nora's testimony.

> Q. This will, Miss Harrington. Can you tell us about the circumstances under which it was signed and witnessed?
>
> A. Yes, sir. We'd finished dinner—it was about nine o'clock that night—the second of July, was it?—and Aunt Hannah asked if Mr. Holton and I would come into her study to witness her signature on a document. We went into the study and there was a typed sheet of paper on her desk. Through the window we could see Danny Lipton mowing the lawn and she called to Jay—John Tuttle—to ask Mr. Lipton to come inside and be a witness, too. Jay went out and got Danny, and then Jay went off somewhere, and Aunt Hannah explained to the three of us that she'd just written a new will, changing a few small details in the former one. She wanted me to sign, too, she said, just in case three signatures proved necessary in a home-drawn will.

"Lies, Joe," I said indignantly. "Lies, every word, Joe. How did they persuade her to say all this?"

"Hold on," Joe said, "there's more, and all of it equally interesting."

> Q. But did you not find it odd that Mrs. Meerloo's will had been changed to include John Tuttle as beneficiary?

140

A. Well, of course I had no way of knowing at the time that she'd done this, sir. She didn't show me the will, or tell me what was in it. But she was very fond of Jay, and very proud of him. He'd graduated Phi Beta Kappa and magna cum laude from Union College, and he was doing splendidly in graduate school. I think she looked on him as something of the son she'd never had.

Q. So you feel no bitterness that in this will—constructed without a lawyer—she reduced your own personal legacy by a third, which, in an estate this size, represented a great deal of money?

A. Well, sir, it was Aunt Hannah's money, and her wish, obviously. How could I be bitter?

Q. Your cousin Robert Gruble has suggested that John Tuttle may have used undue influence upon your aunt, Miss Harrington. I would like now to ask you—and remind you at the same time that you are under oath: you were in the house at the time that your aunt conceived the will, and you witnessed her signing of the will. Did John Tuttle at any time use undue influence—any persuasion of any kind—on your aunt, to encourage this change in her will?

A. No, sir. Absolutely not, sir.

Q. Thank you, Miss Harrington.

"Phew," I whistled, sinking back into the pillows. Nora's testimony just happened to end at the bottom of a page and I sat there digesting once and for all the fact that Hannah's niece had been in the house all the time, and therefore must have known what was happening upstairs to her aunt. In 1965 she had submitted to verifying and even enlarging upon Holton's testimony, and she had done so under oath. By what means had they kept her from going to the police instead?

Joe said soberly, "This is the sleight-of-hand you predicted, Amelia, right here in the transcript we'rereading. The magic trick they pulled out of their hats: Nora."

I said incredulously, "If it weren't for Hannah's note in the hurdy-gurdy, Joe—it all sounds so *plausible,* and yet we know that every damn word is a lie."

I sat bolt upright as another fact struck me. "Joe," I gasped, "Joe, if every word about the signing and witnessing of this will is a lie, then do you realize it's possible that Hannah never met Hubert Holton at dinner on July 2, *and may never have met Holton at all?*"

Joe whistled. "Not bad, Amelia. Sleight-of-hand is right."

I said with growing excitement, "Wipe it all out, Joe, and Danny Lipton was *not* mowing the lawn that evening around nine o'clock. He was *not* called in on the spur of the moment. Hannah did *not* invite anyone to her study to witness the signing of a will. And Holton, besides *not* spending that evening with Hannah talking about books and politics, was never invited to stay for the weekend."

"You realize," Joe said grimly, "what that makes of Holton, don't you?"

I nodded, pleased. *"One of the faceless ones!"*

Joe was silent and then he said softly, "It makes sense, you know, it makes a frightening kind of sense. Someone unknown to Hannah, someone unfamiliar, and we have only their word for it that Holton was the man who came to dinner and charmed Hannah." He shook his head. "Maybe we've been going about this backward, Amelia. Maybe we should have begun by finding out exactly what happened to each of these people after they murdered Hannah. Daniel Lipton had his throat cut by persons unknown five months later. . . . Nora's in a hospital and has been for years. . . . I'd certainly be interested in knowing what's happened to John Tuttle and Hubert Holton, wouldn't you?"

"But what about Nora?" I demanded. "Joe, I've met her—"

"In a psychiatric hospital," he pointed out dryly.

I brushed this aside. "Of course something tragic happened to her back in 1965. That's obvious. What I want to know, Joe, is *what*. What did they do to her, what hold did they have over her?"

Joe scowled. "The one point in her favor—and there aren't many, Amelia—is that she lost a great deal of money by the change in wills and by her aunt's death."

"And the second point in her favor," I pointed out indignantly, "is that she spent every summer of her life with her aunt, Joe—willingly—and she had to have *cared*."

"I wonder what this John Tuttle was like," mused Joe. "We've only Hubert Holton's description of him as a brilliant student and a charming substitute son to Hannah, but he was also a boy who grew up in an orphanage with no money, apparently no Tuttle relatives who would claim him—and with all the Tuttles around *that* must have stung—and so no family. He was an outsider, an outcast, and yet somehow he ends up with about $700,000, Amelia. That's a lot of money."

"Which means," I said cynically, "that he could very well have been charming and brilliant. Or clever."

Joe reached for the phone beside the bed. "There's one person we've not reached yet, and that's Mrs. Morneau."

"Her testimony comes next," I said, glancing down

143

at the records, and he put down the phone, waiting. "And very cautious and wary it sounds, Joe."

I read:

Q. Did you know Mr. Hubert Holton?

A. No, sir. I said before I'd heard the name somewhere, and I've remembered now. When John Tuttle was away at his college he'd write Miss Hannah a letter now and then and she'd mention how taken Jay was with this one professor, Mr. Holton, and how nice it was this professor had taken an interest in Jay. But know him, no sir.

Q. Would you describe for us, please, the relationship that Mr. John Tuttle had with your employer Mrs. Meerloo?

A. He was always very charming with her, sir.

Q. Did Mrs. Meerloo, before you left for your vacation, which I believe was on July 1, mention the possibility of a new will to you, or did you overhear any mention of it?

A. No, sir. And I can't say as I understand it, sir, because Mr. Garwin Mason was her lawyer and so far as I know he was right there in his office in town.

Q. Yet you do identify this as Mrs. Meerloo's signature?

A. Oh yes, sir, it's hers just like the two men here testified. Those two experts. Just the same as on all the checks she signed when she paid me.

Q. Did you have occasion to visit the house after your departure on July 1, or to

144

speak with Mrs. Meerloo by telephone perhaps?

A. No, sir. I did call twice, both times on the Fourth of July, in the afternoon it was, just before I left for New Hampshire to visit my friends. I phoned to tell her there'd be fireworks in Anglesworth that night—she always loved fireworks—but there wasn't any answer.

Q. Did you find that unusual?

A. I didn't think about it much, sir. It was a lovely day, the weather was hot and Miss Nora was a great one for picnics. Mrs. Meerloo always looked forward to July, when Miss Nora and Mr. Robin visited her.

Q. And would you say it was typical of Mrs. Meerloo to invite Mr. Holton to be a house guest for a month in place of Mr. Robert Gruble?

A. (unintelligible)

Q. Speak up, Mrs. Morneau.

A. Well, I can't say she'd done anything like that before. She was a—well, a very private person, sir. Enjoyed a quiet life. She wrote her stories, you know, and she—well, meditated is what she called it, something she learned on her travels. She must have thought Mr. Holton would be company for Miss Nora, for tennis and the like, what with Mr. Robin being stuck in New York this year, although she usually played tennis with Jay. Mr. Tuttle, that is.

Q. Would you say, in your estimation, Mrs. Morneau, that Mr. John Tuttle ever

used any undue influence upon Mrs. Meerloo?

A. Well, he had the run of the house, you
might say. He wasn't a real chauffeur, not
in the usual way, sir. It's not the sort of thing
I understand, "undue influence." Up to the
time I left nothing was any different from
before.

Q. Thank you, Mrs. Morneau.

I told Joe, seeing his hand still on the telephone,
"You might as well wait for Daniel Lipton's testimony,
too."

"Anything there?"

"Proof that he was in on it, too," I told him, glancing
over his testimony. "He says that he was mowing the
lawn that evening, was called in to witness and sign
a will, and Mrs. Meerloo gave him five dollars for it."

Joe snorted. "And we know that was a bloody lie."

"But they did such a good job," I said softly. "All of
them. They make it sound so believable, Joe."

"Because they were in collusion and their futures
were at stake," Joe pointed out. "Let's hope that Danny
Lipton received more than five dollars for perjuring
himself, because five months later he certainly ran out
of a future."

I said, frowning, "I think he did more than perjure
himself, Joe, I think he must have been the other 'faceless one.' Hannah wouldn't know him that well, would
she? His walk, his gestures—Holton could have done
any talking that was necessary."

"Go on," Joe said, watching me. "How do you see it?"

"I don't *know*, of course," I said, "because we haven't
caught up with John Tuttle or Mr. Holton yet, but
everything points to their having plotted this out together. How they bought Nora's silence we don't know
yet, but I think they were waiting for Mrs. Morneau

to leave on her vacation, and as soon as she left Hubert Holton moved into the house and Danny Lipton, too. They just—moved in." There were tears in my eyes as I pictured it. "And just before they arrived Hannah walked into the box room, the door was locked behind her—did you notice the lock is still on the outside of that door, Joe?—and she became literally a prisoner in her own house. *Not* on a happy July Fourth picnic, as Mrs. Morneau supposed, but hidden away in a hot little room without food or water."

"Steady there," Joe said gently. "Before you get too carried away, grab that phone book and look up John Tuttle's name, will you? It's time we find him. I suggest we telephone every John Tuttle in the book and see if we can zero in on the one who graduated from Union College in the early sixties. I'll do the calling. I'll say I'm an alumnus or something. Look up Holton, too, and see if he's around still."

I had already turned to the H's. "No Holtons listed," I told him. I turned to the T's and winced. "Good heavens there are dozens upon *dozens* of Tuttles, nearly a whole page of them."

Joe, watching my face, said, "So? What's the matter?"

"Damn," I said bitterly. "I will read to you herewith all the J. Tuttles listed in this blasted county directory. *County*, Joe. As follows: Jacque Tuttle. Three James Tuttles. Jane Tuttle. Jason Tuttle. Jaspar Tuttle. Jared Tuttle. Jean Tuttle. Jebediah Tuttle. Jerry Tuttle. Jess Tuttle. Jim Tuttle. Joel Tuttle. Joseph P. Tuttle, Joseph M. Tuttle, Joseph A. Tuttle and Joseph L. Tuttle. Jules Tuttle. Justinian Tuttle."

"Not a John among them?"

"Not a one," I told him, and presented him with the directory to prove it.

147

He scanned it unbelievingly. "Incredible—there are always Johns."

"So one is led to believe."

He tossed the directory to the floor, picked up the phone, and dialed the number I'd scribbled on paper yesterday. "We need Mrs. Morneau more than ever," he said. "Let's hope she's at home finally. At the least she can tell us where to find Tuttle."

Apparently Mrs. Morneau was at home, and while Joe made an appointment for us to see her after lunch I read the opinion filed by Judge Arthur Pomeroy in December of 1965, IN RE WILL OF HANNAH GRUBLE MEER-LOO. There was a lengthy analysis of Undue Influence, with references to Barnes *vs.* Barnes, 66 Me. 286,297 (1876) and Rogers, Appellant, 123 Me. 123 A. 634 (1924) but I skimmed through these to read the last paragraph:

> We cannot know (wrote the judge) what circumstances led Mrs. Meerloo to write a will of her own making on the second of July, 1965, when all previous wills had been drawn by her attorney. But this is her signature, testified to by two experts as well as by those familiar with her signature and style of writing. The will was also witnessed by three people, among them her niece Leonora Harrington, a relative of obvious closeness to the legatee, who was present at the signing of this will, and has testified so under oath. It is a legal will, and must therefore be honored and allowed to pass through Probate.

To this was appended the message that the appellant, Robert Gruble, was denied his application to have counsel fees paid out of the estate.

On the bottom of the page someone had written in ink: decision made by R. Gruble not to appeal.

I wondered why.

I thought, they could never have gotten away with this without Nora's testifying for them.

And this, I realized, was the hell that Nora had faced each morning since July 25, 1965.

10

Mrs. Morneau had said she would see us at one o'clock.
It was half-past eleven when we finished reading the
Probate Court records, and we had just decided on an
early, leisurely lunch when the telephone rang. It was
strange hearing it ring in a motel room hundreds of
miles from home.

"Oh no," groaned Joe, and picked up the receiver.
"Osbourne here." He listened and I saw his face tighten.
"For God's sake, Ken, I'm way up here in Maine, you
know, couldn't they have decided this earlier? . . . Yes,
I know, I know, but this is Tuesday, they had all day
yesterday and I can't believe they didn't know . . . Christ.
Okay, Ken, I don't know *how* but—right. Okay."

He hung up and sat down hard on the bed. "Damn. You heard?"

"When do you have to go?" I asked, my heart plunging.

"I've got to be in court at nine tomorrow morning."

I stared at him in astonishment. "In Trafton? But you'll need a plane, and we don't even know if there's an airport, do we?"

The next forty minutes were spent on the telephone. I didn't even have time to think about Hannah, or court records, or how I would have to drive back to Trafton alone in the van. There was one direct flight out of Bangor for New York each day, but it had already left. There was a flight from Bangor to Boston but too late to connect with the six o'clock plane to New York. We were referred to Blue Harbor Airlines. They had one seat available on a plane leaving for Boston at four o'clock that would connect with the flight to New York at six, which would connect with a New York flight to Trafton at nine, arriving at half-past ten. I hadn't realized how far from home we were. While we waited for the airline to call back and confirm all these reservations I must say that our conversation turned hilariously prosaic.

I would have to drive home alone in the van, Joe reminded me, and he wanted my promise that I would leave for Trafton first thing in the morning, the earlier the better, and no nonsense about it.

I promised.

He didn't at all appreciate leaving me here, he said, pacing the room furiously, and he wanted my promise that after we visited Mrs. Morneau, and after I'd delivered him to the airport, I would consider all investigations into Hannah's death suspended. Done with. Finished. Promise?

I promised.

I was to drive no faster than fifty miles per hour on the highway, he said sternly; he would mark my route on the map and I was not to attempt too much driving in one day, or get too tired, did I understand?

It was really very endearing but I was glad when the airlines clerk called back to confirm space on all three flights. We just had time to buy two packages of peanut butter crackers in the coffee shop and to review en route to Mrs. Morneau's the questions we wanted to ask, and the tact with which we must ask them: a biography would again be our cover.

With the help of the map I'd bought we found Farnsworth Road. Number 23 was a trim little white Cape Cod house with a picket fence around it, a gate, and a neat little flagstone walk leading up to the front door, which was painted yellow to match the shutters. Everything was very neat, even to the hand-printed name over the mailbox. We rang the bell and the door was opened by Mrs. Morneau. She had a pale, placid face, scarcely lined at all, gray eyes, and iron-gray hair forced into a very neat, stern bun at the nape of her neck. Her figure was what would be called full, and so sternly, rigidly corseted that it thrust out her bosom like a tray.

At sight of us she said, "I didn't expect you to be so young." Her voice held a note of sharpness in it.

"Well," I pointed out, smiling, "Hannah Gruble's book was for young people, you know. Mr. Osbourne here is thirty-one. And I'm Amelia Jones, by the way."

We shook hands. "She gave me a copy, autographed," Mrs. Morneau said, and, apparently forgiving us our youth, allowed us entry. We followed her into a neat, boxlike living room with so many knickknacks on shelves and tables that I could only suppose they were installed to keep her busy dusting them. We sat down, Joe and I on the couch by the fireplace, Mrs. Morneau opposite us, very erect in a chair with wooden arms, her feet placed primly together on the floor. "Imagine a book being written about her," she said in an awed voice. "After all these years, too. Of course I knew it was a fine book, but still—I hear you can't buy it any more in the shops."

I felt a pang of guilt and temporized by thinking that perhaps, given a few English courses, I might one day write Hannah's biography; after all, I'd never imagined that I'd own the Ebbtide Shop. I brought out my spiral notebook, laid it professionally on my lap and dug out my pen. "You worked for Mrs. Meerloo a long time, Mrs. Morneau?"

"Oh yes, miss. Ever since she came to Carleton and bought the place on Tuttle Road. You understand she knew how to housekeep very well herself—she'd been born poor, she told me—but she left it all to me. Not one of these women like some," she added with a sniff, "who go sneaking around seeing if there's dust on the mantel. She couldn't have cared less. An angel she was to work for, I can tell you."

"You were very fond of her then," Joe said.

"Fond?" Mrs. Morneau approached the word warily. "All I know is, when I heard she'd died I couldn't stop crying for hours, which is more than I can say for my own father's passing, heaven rest his soul. And though she did leave me a rare amount of money—well, it seems you need only get money to learn it don't amount to much if it leaves you alone. I'd gladly give it all back, every penny of it, to have things as they used to be." Her voice turned nostalgic. "Just her and me living there together and the children coming summers. Her writing in her room or sitting cross-legged on the floor doing her thinking, or saying 'Jane, it's time we had baklava, don't you think?' She was very partial to baklava, she was."

153

"You must be a fine cook," said Joe encouragingly.

"Good enough for Miss Hannah anyway," she said, and turned her attention to the table beside her. "Hearing you was coming," she said, "I went looking for pictures and found a few. You might be interested." Her voice was careless, a little too casual, and at once I realized two things: one, that I didn't want to see a picture of Hannah, because I had my own picture of her, inside of me, and two, that in the interval between Joe's phone call and our arrival Mrs. Morneau had begun writing her own scenario. Already she was seeing herself as Someone Who Had Known the Great, a high priestess dispensing anecdotes of Hannah. Perhaps she even envisioned herself being interviewed on radio or television. "Hannah used to feel," she would say, or "I remember so well the way she . . ."

She handed me two snapshots and a faded cardboard photograph, saying, "I'm sure there are more but these might look well in your book."

"But that will come later," I told her, smiling, "after the book is complete, and then I believe there are arrangements."

She understood the word arrangements, and nodded, looking hopeful.

I glanced reluctantly at the photographs. The stiff cardboard photo was Hannah's wedding picture, clear but taken at a distance. I saw a thin, slight girl in a long, old-fashioned dress standing next to a tall young man in an army uniform and cap. They looked very young, very happy and a little frightened. I turned to the second picture, a close-up dated 1950, and realized how characterless the first picture was, for here was Hannah years later: a small oval face, grave dark eyes with the hint of a smile lurking in their depths; odd, slanted black brows that were no more than a quick deft brush stroke over the eyes; a small chin, mouth

154

and nose. As Garwin Mason had said, nothing particularly distinctive at first glance, except for those strange eyebrows. . . . The third snapshot showed a slender figure sitting cross-legged under a tree, reading a book.

"Thank you," I said, grateful that they in no way threatened my own picture of Hannah. "And by the way," I added as I handed them over to Joe to see, "before we begin, we've heard that Mrs. Meerloo completed a new book just before her death. Would you know anything about that?"

"Ah, that would be Mr. Mason," she said, nodding. "He's the one insisted there was a book, for it's nothing I knew about. Him being co-executor of the estate, and Mr. Robin being busy in New York, it was him and me searched the house for it."

"And you found nothing?"

"Not so much as a scrap."

I shook my head sadly. "Well—one question we have," I said, putting that aside reluctantly. "Mrs. Meerloo gave so much money to her projects but we can't find any record of the Jason Meerloo Orphanage. Is it still in existence?"

A faint shadow crossed her face. "No'm," she said stiffly. "It went bankrupt in 1970, and that would have broken Miss Hannah's heart, I can tell you. The state took it over and the children were moved to Bangor to an orphanage there."

"I understand John Tuttle, her chauffeur, came from the orphanage when it existed?" I asked.

"Yes'm," she said.

Joe intervened, his voice smooth as silk. "Could you tell us at what point Mrs. Meerloo became interested in John Tuttle—her protégé, as he was called in her will?"

She looked startled. "So you've read the will, have

155

you? Well, I had to look up that word protégé in the dictionary, I did, my husband being the French one, and me a Pritchett. Means 'one under the protection and care of another,' it does."

"That sounds about right," Joe said encouragingly.

"Not to me," she said sternly. "Miss Hannah was not one to treat any of the orphans different from the other. Each summer she hired one of 'em—sometimes two— to do her yard-work, those who wanted spending money. And when they reached high school age there'd be one of them to stay in the apartment over the garage and drive her car for her. Jay—that's what John Tuttle was called—was no different, at least not at first. Of course he was the brightest youngster there—they had those IQ tests, you know, and she'd lend him books. Big heavy ones. He never came to the house, though, until he was twelve or thirteen. First he cut grass for her and burned leaves in the autumn, although I will say they talked about books and plays and things a lot on the porch. He had a good mind, Miss Hannah used to say. When he got his driver's license he began driving for her summers—he was a junior in high school then—and after that she helped him send off his college application, and of course she paid all his bills at college and saw to it he had the same kind of clothes Mr. Robin wore, and pocket money. In that way he was treated different, although she did send one of the girls to fashion design school for two years, and another boy to vocational school."

"Very generous," Joe murmured.

"So he was there at the house," I said, "when Nora and Robin came summers?"

"Nora and Robin," she echoed, and sighed. "Seems so natural to hear them names, and so long ago, too. Such a pretty little thing Nora was, a real beauty."

"Which of them chose the words for the gravestone in the cemetery?" I asked.

"Strange words, aren't they," she said. "Mr. Robin did that."

I like you for that, Robin, I thought. "And did they get along well together summers?" I asked. "The three of them—Nora, Robin, and John Tuttle?"

"Children do," she said vaguely.

"Later as well?" prodded Joe. "When they were no longer children?"

Mrs. Morneau began to look troubled; I could see that these questions were in conflict with the private scenario she'd written. She must have imagined herself telling us what foods Hannah liked best, and what colors she loved, and how the household was run. The idea of relationships was unsettling to her, and I wondered for the first time what might have happened to Mr. Morneau. Perhaps a lifetime of dusting surfaces was infectious, and surfaces were all that she acknowledged.

"How did Mrs. Meerloo feel about John Tuttle?" asked Joe.

"Oh, very pleased," said Mrs. Morneau primly. "He turned out so well, you know. Very bright. She always hated waste."

"And may we ask your own personal impression of him?"

Her face stiffened. "You'd do better asking someone else, for I thought he took too many liberties and told Miss Hannah so myself. But she'd only shake her head over me and remind me I went to church regularly every Sunday. Stigma—that was the word she used. Because he was an orphanage boy."

Mrs. Morneau had not liked John Tuttle. Jealousy, I wondered? The resentment of a native over a local

157

boy being given special status? I remembered to scribble a few doodles to look professional, and then I cleared my throat and began again. "What we're looking for just now, Mrs. Morneau—we've pretty much sketched in all the facts and reached her death—"

"Oh, tragic that was," Mrs. Morneau interrupted fiercely. "So young to go. Not to you two young people, of course, but people around here live to their seventies and eighties and sometimes into their nineties and I can tell you, forty is young to die, as you'll find out soon enough."

"Yes, I'm sure of that, Mrs. Morneau," I told her. "And we're delighted to have found you, you're going to be an invaluable source of material for us, and I'm sure you won't mind our consulting you from time to time—"

"Oh, any time at all," Mrs. Morneau said eagerly; this was obviously what she wanted to hear.

"But for the moment we hoped—and we wondered if you could help us here—we'd like to talk with the people who were with her during the three weeks before her tragic accident."

"Oh," said Mrs. Morneau.

"Interviews," pointed out Joe, "with the last people who saw her."

"Oh," repeated Mrs. Morneau, and suddenly the expressions that had enlivened her placid face were called back inside of her like children at dusk; shutters closed and I could hear them snap. She folded her hands in her lap, her lips thinned and she said, "Well, I don't know about that."

"There was this man, a house guest, Mr. Hubert Holton—"

She nodded. "It comes back to me how excited Jay was about meeting that man. Nora, too."

"Nora?" I said quickly. "Nora met him before that summer?"

She made a vague gesture with her hands. "Visiting Jay at his college, you know. Dances, homecoming weekends. Not often but sometimes."

I met Joe's startled glance and looked quickly away before Mrs. Morneau noticed. "Do you know where we can reach Mr. Holton?" I asked. "And John Tuttle was there that July, too."

She said warily, "They were there, yes. So they said. And Miss Nora."

"We've already spoken with Miss Nora."

That surprised her. "Oh?" she said, and gave me a furtive glance. "You've been to the hospital?"

"Yes." I shook my head. "It's very sad, isn't it?"

"I can only say," announced Mrs. Morneau, disapproval bringing her back to life, "that it's a blessing Miss Hannah never knew, although they do say the dead can see us sometimes, don't they? But then Miss Nora was always frail—frail inside, not like Miss Hannah who could stand up to life, for she'd had her share of tragedies, I can tell you. After she inherited her aunt's money Miss Nora had a beautiful house built near the water—half glass I heard it was, which cost a pretty penny. But bewildered she looked when I saw her six months later, and a year later she looked frightened. Of being alone I think it was, and I should have known then, for she wasn't too steady on her feet. Drinking too much, you see. Frail she was," Mrs. Morneau repeated with the pride of one who had survived. "Always frail."

Mrs. Morneau's confidences seemed to come in spasms. I said firmly, "We've tried to find John Tuttle in the telephone book—"

Mrs. Morneau stared at me in astonishment and

then she threw back her head and laughed. "Him? You won't find any John Tuttle in the phone book, miss. Changed his name he did. Changed a lot of things, including his name."

"To what?" I asked, trying not to sound eager.

But Mrs. Morneau's face darkened again; she looked from me to Joe and then back again. "You'd go to him and say Jane Morneau told you where to find him, I expect." Her voice had become harder now; I wondered if she'd become suspicious of us at this turn of the conversation. "That wouldn't do," she said. "That wouldn't do at all." she looked at her watch, a very neat, plain gold band on her plump wrist. "I think we really have to continue this another time," she said, "for I've work to do now. I've spoken enough." She rose to her feet, and stood over us, massive and implacable.

Rising, I said, "You won't tell us where to find John Tuttle?"

She shook her head. "I'm sorry, Miss—Jones, is it? I can't help you."

Joe, rising too, said with a smile, "Surely then you can tell us how to locate Mr. Holton?"

She shook her head even more firmly. "Any questions about Miss Hannah I'll be glad to answer but that's all I can say. Anything else—ask Miss Nora," she said almost maliciously.

"I see," I said, following her helplessly to the door. "We can appreciate your reticence, of course, but you must know—that is, if only—"

"We've come a long way to interview John Tuttle as well as you," Joe put in sternly.

We were at the door now. She held her tightly corseted figure so straight that I feared for a moment that she might snap in two. She said in a harsh voice, looking straight at me and ignoring Joe, "There's no bringing Miss Hannah back, miss. Or Danny Lipton who

160

had his throat cut on Christmas Eve that same year, or Miss Nora either, who's as good as gone. The dead are dead. It's the living—" Her voice broke and she added flatly, "I don't want anyone thinking I gossip, miss, it would be best if you send any questions by letter and not come here again."

With this she closed the door in our faces.

Joe took my arm but I shook my head. "Listen," I whispered, because from the other side of the door came small retching sounds; I realized that Mrs. Morneau was crying, or trying not to but unable to suppress her hard angry sobs. Just as abruptly the sounds stopped and footsteps fled down the hall.

We walked slowly and thoughtfully down the walk to the van and climbed inside. As Joe started the engine I said, "Joe, we frightened Mrs. Morneau."

He nodded. "Badly."

I looked back at the trim white bungalow with its yellow shutters and picket fence; I thought I saw her face at the window and I waved reassuringly, but as the van moved down the street the face vanished. "She suspects the truth then, Joe? Or guesses?"

Joe said, "I think she was trying to explain herself at the very end. We hadn't mentioned Daniel Lipton but she pointed out that he's dead and Nora's as good as dead."

"So obviously John Tuttle is the threat," I said, drawing a deep breath. "She didn't say that *he's* dead."

"It's a nice little house," Joe pointed out. "Mortgage-free, I should imagine. Thirty-five thousand went a lot further in 1965 than it does now. She probably bought her house for ten or twelve thousand, invested the rest, and is living very well in her frugal way. If John Tuttle is the one who wrote that last will of Hannah's he saw to it that Mrs. Morneau didn't get cheated, which was certainly shrewd of him. He cut out Greenacres and

161

the orphanage and everything else, but he didn't cut out Mrs. Morneau and I'm sure she got the point. It was a subtle form of pay-off. She's safe as long as she doesn't rock the boat."

"But you're implying that she knew from the beginning!" I said.

Joe shook his head. "No, I'm not. All I'm saying is that she knows a good many things about the people involved in this that she doesn't want to tell us, details we've not learned yet, and I think over the years these have crept up on her, she noticed discrepancies and reached certain conclusions she's tried to repress. I don't believe she consciously admits there was murder, or even could have been. She just feels frightened and edgy about it all. But damn it, we didn't get much from her, Amelia."

"Yes, we did," I protested. "We learned that John Tuttle has changed his name and that Mrs. Morneau is frightened."

"But we don't know to what name he changed it. Or why Robin never appealed that Probate Court verdict."

"Ah, you noticed that too?" I said, pleased. "That leaves three questions dangling: who is Tuttle now, where is Holton, and why there was no appeal."

"Amelia, am I heading in the right direction for the airport?"

I picked up the map, glanced at it and nodded. "At the next intersection keep straight; it's about nine miles farther. Joe, I have the court records to return to Garwin Mason before I leave tomorrow, and I'm sure he could tell us about John Tuttle. If," I added cheekily, "I can solicit your permission for one more inquiry?"

"Don't push me, Amelia," he said crossly. "Go to Mason but if he doesn't want to tell you, put it in the hands of that detective across the street from me in Trafton."

"Zebroski?" I said, remembering his garish sign.

"Yes. And then turn it over to the police."

That sounded reasonable, we were nearing the end, anyway. "Why are you suddenly cross?" I asked.

"Because if it weren't for the van I'd kidnap you and take you back with me on the plane."

"There's only one seat available," I reminded him.

"I don't like leaving you."

I didn't particularly like being left but I thought it would be a good chance to gain a sense of perspective. I mean, in the space of four and a half days a great deal had happened to me, and I could see that some stabilization might be therapeutic. Was I, for instance, still me? Could I still function alone, or was my confidence going to collapse as soon as Joe left? I remembered that originally I had planned to take this trip alone, which seemed inconceivable to me now.

The airport was a far cry from La Guardia. We bumped over a dirt road to a parking lot surrounding a wooden building, parked the van, and walked into a room with long wooden benches and a tiny counter. Out by the hangar in the back a few small planes sat like swollen birds. A bearded young man dozed in one corner, his feet on his dufflebag. While Joe paid for his ticket I read the same ubiquitous political posters: VOTE FOR SILAS WHITNEY! VOTE FOR ANGUS TUTTLE! but I was spared any photographs this time. A noisy family of six arrived, followed by a well-dressed businessman with an attaché case. The businessman wore huge round spectacles and appeared singularly out of place. As if aware of this he was careful not to look at anyone.

In the interests of seeing Garwin Mason before he left his office I kissed Joe good-by as soon as he'd bought his ticket, and resolutely walked out without looking back. I shed a few tears as I drove away, watching myself like a hawk for any more dubious forms of grief. "Forty-eight hours, Amelia," I reminded myself. "You'll be back in Trafton in forty-eight hours and it's no big deal, right?"

Wrong. I was going to have to keep very busy.

It was at this moment, driving down the highway and still brooding over Joe's departure, that one of those crazy thunderbolts interrupted my thoughts to prove how industriously the subconscious works over puzzles long after they've been put aside. I mean, I know quite a lot about the subconscious because once therapy started opening me up, it was amazing the dreams that surfaced to explain what had happened to me and how I'd really felt about things; it was like a little box that had recorded everything I'd forgotten or couldn't understand. Now there slipped into my mind four small words from Hannah's letter that I'd never really noticed.

Hannah had written, "I will hide this somewhere in a dif-

ferent place and perhaps someday someone will find it."

In a different place.

Different from *what* place?

I'd read the letter dozens of times, and so had Joe, and I'd skimmed over the phrase assuming she'd meant the hurdy-gurdy was a "different" kind of place in which to conceal a note, as indeed it was. Now I found myself looking at these four words from a new angle, as if I were inside of the mind that wrote them, and from this angle it seemed a very curious phrase to use unless Hannah had *already hidden something else.* I saw it as four words written without awareness or intention, a trick of Hannah's thought processes that insisted on accuracy. It suddenly meant to me "I will not hide it in the same place."

I put my foot down on the gas pedal and roared into the parking area of the Golden Kingfisher Motel, raced into unit 18, and fumbled through my papers for a copy of Hannah's note. The words were waiting for me, I hadn't imagined them: my subconscious had known they were there all along. I stood with the note in my hand and thought about this carefully. I was remembering the length of time that Hannah had been locked in that room, long enough to acquaint her very well with all its corners and to learn its hiding places. What might she have wanted to conceal from the "faceless ones" as soon as she realized that she was a prisoner?

Garwin Mason had stated firmly that Hannah's second book had been completed. Because it had never been found I had leaped to the conclusion that Hannah's murderers must have destroyed the manuscript. Could she possibly have been carrying *In the Land of the Golden Warriors* with her when she entered the box room, and hidden it there?

It all depended, of course, on just how she'd been lured there in the first place, which was something I'd not thought about before. Considering it now, however, I couldn't conceive of John Tuttle enticing her there because she would have known, then, that he was involved. It seemed to me quite logical to suppose that she'd gone there of her own volition: to get something out of a trunk, perhaps? Was it where she did some of her writing, or did she use the room for what Mrs. Morneau called her "thinking" and her meditating? The latter seemed to hold the more potential: the room was too hot for working but it was dim and quiet, far removed from the distracting sounds in the house. It would have been a very *good* place for meditating.

What else could she have possibly concealed earlier, before she hid her letter in the hurdy-gurdy?

The contrary part of me pointed out that she might have wanted to hide an extremely valuable diamond ring that she wore on her finger. Or an heirloom pin.

"No," I said, shaking my head, "I know Hannah now

165

and she wouldn't have considered jewelry important enough to hide. With all her money she chose privacy and simplicity, I doubt that she even wore jewelry."

"Well, she certainly wouldn't go around carrying a manuscript with her," retorted that perverse self.

"Why not?" I asked. "It's a large house, she might have carried it the way some women carry around their knitting, or she might have been planning to work on it as soon as she left the box room."

"And have hidden it where?" asked that other me.

"Exactly," I said out loud, and felt the first lift of excitement. There was the bureau, for one thing, which I'd given only a cursory inspection. I was sure it was the same bureau, never removed, for who would want to refurbish a box room? There was also the filthy old mattress, so full of craters and hills that it must have lain there for years; and there was the floor. I hadn't looked for any loose floor boards, it hadn't even occurred to me until now.

The possibilities were fragile but my hopes were rising; I had convinced myself now that Hannah had hidden the sequel in the box room. It might no longer be there but I knew with absolute certainty that I couldn't leave for Trafton in the morning without looking for it. Even the remotest possibility of finding an unpublished Gruble manuscript—the missing sequel to *The Maze in the Heart of the Castle*—left me shaken. If it was there—poor Joe, I thought, to miss such a triumph!

I glanced at my watch. It was nearly four o'clock and I'd promised Joe that I'd leave early tomorrow. I didn't think I'd be able to find Bob Tuttle in his real estate office at this hour and, even if I did, I wondered how I could possibly explain my interest in taking apart the box room. I sat down on the bed and thought about this problem, and of course there was only one solution, which I accepted very calmly.

166

11

I drove first to a hardware store and purchased what I needed, and then I headed for Carleton, conscientiously remaining inside the speed limit to please Joe. I passed Simon Pritchett's General Store, veered right at the intersection on to Tuttle Road, and turned into the driveway of Hannah's house. I drove the car across the grass and around to the rear, out of sight, and cut the engine. Climbing out, I grasped the flashlight and the tool kit I'd bought, and prepared to burgle Hannah's house.

Morally I felt relatively sanguine about committing this illegal act, for the crusading spirit was high in me and I thought that if pressed hard I could always buy the house, although all I wanted from it was a manuscript. But I soon discovered certain practical drawbacks to the tidy professional job I'd planned. For one thing the wind was rising in that insistent and menacing way that suggests a brewing thunderstorm, and the back door, which I'd considered removing by unscrewing its hinges, was over-sized and built for the ages. Expediency won: after studying the situation I simply broke one of the small panes of glass in the door and reached inside to unbolt the lock. I told myself that, if I recovered a sequel to Hannah's book, Bob Tuttle might forgive my larceny but just in case he didn't see things my way I would place ten dollars in an envelope and mail it to him in the morning.

Once inside the house the cold hit me like a fist, a flat damp cold that had been building for eight months and needed more than a few warm days to dispel. I was surprised at the difference that companions had made on my earlier visit. For instance, as I left the kitchen and passed the door to the cellar, I could feel prickles run up and down my spine as if four murderers walked behind me, and at any moment I might hear Hannah's scream. The house was not at all quiet, either; every board that I put a foot on sent out a small groan of protest in the cold, and the wind outside wrapped itself around the exterior and made whispery moaning sounds. I hurried up the staircase to the second floor and here I found it so dark that I had to turn on my flashlight: I didn't like this, either. Only one thought kept me going: Hannah's manuscript *In the Land of the Golden Warriors,* and what Joe would say if I found it after all these years. It would certainly be a smashing denouement to our trip north. I could picture his explosion—"Amelia, you *promised*!"—and then his quick, marvelous smile, a hug, a kiss and about three minutes of intense questioning during which I would be given a few hints as to how wonderful I was, how intelligent, and how clever.

I opened the door to the attic and propped it wide with a brick in spite of its having neither lock nor key. I walked up the several steps to the box room, which Bob Tuttle had left unlocked, and opened the door and walked in, closing it behind me to shut out the darkness and the sounds of wind.

Hannah, I said silently, *I've come back.*

It was dim and silent in here; I switched on my flashlight and placed it on the bureau, and then with the screwdriver I'd brought I began to remove the rear panel of the bureau. This didn't take long because the back had been made of cheap wood that began to splinter before I'd removed two of its screws. I felt a little foolish when it was done: the bureau was quite simply a bureau, and empty at that.

Carrying the flashlight with me I went down on my hands and knees and started examining the wide oak floor boards, but I succeeded only in adding a decade of dust to my skirt and hands. The floor had been well made and I couldn't even find a squeaky board or a telltale scratch. With a sigh I gave up on the floor as a repository and turned my attention to the bed. I pulled aside the flannel cover to the mattress and ran my hands over its break-neck lines: there were holes, bulges, and a complete redistribution of whatever cheap mattresses are stuffed with: an atrocious thing to lie on. My hands explored every deviation; I turned the mattress over and began again.

Suddenly as I probed a particularly devilish hole in the mattress my fingers encountered resistance down near the foot; there was a difference in texture here, too, from the wads of compacted stuffing I'd groped through. I thought, *It has to be, it has to be, dear God please let it be....* My suspense was so unbearable that

169

I gave up my polite tuggings and feverishly ripped the surface of the mattress into shreds.

And there it was: perhaps two hundred sheets of white paper tightly rolled up and bound by string. I tore off the string, unrolled the pages and saw neatly typed on the first sheet: *In the Land of the Golden Warriors,* by H. M. Gruble.

I had found Hannah's sequel. I was actually holding it in my hands.

I sank down on the remains of the mattress and ran the flashlight over the first few pages. Colin's name occupied almost every paragraph, which delighted me, because Hannah *could* have jumped ahead in time to Colin's children, or chosen another character from the first book, like the prince of Galt, or Serena, but my beloved Colin was here, and apparently only two years older. I couldn't wait to read it. I began eagerly, "One morning in the country of Galt, when the grass was silver with dew and the primroses scarlet in the meadows, a messenger on horseback rode up to Colin's door with a message from the prince. Colin was...."

At that moment I heard the lock on the door to the box room snap with a strange ping! sound, and as I looked up in astonishment a floor board creaked on the landing and I heard the very definite sound of the outer door to the attic closing.

Someone was in the house with me.

I had been in a different world, totally immersed in Hannah's book, and it took a moment to apply intelligence to this improbable discovery. My mind, for instance, absolutely rejected it and yet I noticed that my hands were trembling. My mind told me it was inconceivable that I was not alone; I had entered an empty house, no one had known I was coming here, no one knew that I *was* here, and therefore I was alone. I *had* to be alone.

My senses knew better: my heart was racing and hudding, my hands shaking and I was slowly breaking ut into a cold sweat. I laid aside Hannah's manuscript, iptoed to the door and gently tugged at the knob. It esisted and I pulled harder—very hard—and now here was no doubt about it, I was locked inside. I put ny head against the door and listened. I had the dis-inct feeling that someone was there, and I wondered f he or she were listening on the other side of the door. A faint sound reached my ears that I couldn't quite dentify, a crackling noise, as if someone was crumpling up very stiff paper, and then I heard a floor board creak ome distance away, as of someone leaving. My mind old me that I should call out, scream, shout, there had o have been a mistake, possibly a caretaker or the real state agent checking the house, but my senses told ne to be quiet and think, because I was in grave dan-er.

I am not proud of the several minutes that followed: must have given a great deal of nourishment to Am-nan Singh's demons who feed on violence because my houghts were dark and grim. I paced, wept, and apol-gized profusely to Joe, who must have guessed I might lo something irrational like this. It did not escape me hat my mother had died in an attic and now, irony of ronies, I was to die in an attic, too, and in exactly the oom where Hannah. . . .

But Hannah hadn't died here, I remembered. Nor ad she, I realized, suddenly galvanized by the thought, ossessed a tool kit for breaking and entering.

This punctured my spasm of self-pity. My hysteria ubsided and I crept to the door and listened again to ind out whether anyone was waiting around to learn vhat I'd do. This time there was only silence and I set o work at once. Pulling the bureau over to the door climbed on top of it, carrying screwdriver and hammer, and looked over the possibilities. I found the top hinge of the door and applied my screwdriver to its screws but they'd been painted over so many times that the tool found no leverage. I gave this up and inserted the blade of the screwdriver into the dry wood under the hinge, hammered away at the handle until it prised up one corner of the hinge, and at last saw the hinge pull loose from the wall.

As the door shuddered from the loss of the one hinge I smelled smoke for the first time.

"Smoke!" I cried furiously, and felt my hands begin to shake again.

It was, of course, a very shrewd maneuver to set Hannah's house on fire; there had always been the possibility that the real estate agent would find me before I died of thirst. Obviously I had only an ordinary criminal mind, given to common things like burglary; I lacked the cunning of a killer, and whoever had locked me into the box room wanted me dead. This in itself was a shock.

The smoke, I saw, was seeping lazily in under the door now. I realized that this was the sound I'd heard earlier, not paper but the kindling of a fire somewhere outside, and now the smoke had found me. A very thorough killer, I thought, enraged by his ruthlessness. It seemed a miracle to me now that I'd only broken a glass to get into the house; if he'd known about the tool kit he would never have gone off and left me.

I tore off the scarf around my throat, tied it over my nose and mouth and went to work with a fury on the remaining hinge. When I freed it, the door sagged open, and then nearly fell on top of me as it tore away the lock as well. The landing was thick with smoke. Choking and gagging I grabbed Hannah's manuscript and my purse, found the attic door, and pushed it open Here I nearly fell over the large pile of flaming rags on the threshold. Nothing beyond it appeared to be burning, but the stench of gasoline and smoke set me coughing wildly again. I made one flying leap through the fire and raced for the stairs.

I had taken only two steps down when I heard the crackling noises below, and saw an astonishing brilliance illuminating the walls of the living room. I turned back and raced through the second-story hall until I found a bedroom overlooking the sunporch. I wrenched open a window, unhooked the screen, climbed over the sill, and jumped down to the roof. Here I paused for a better grip on manuscript and purse before I crept to the farthest corner of the roof and jumped again, landing in a bush on the ground and rolling over once. I picked myself up and ran around the corner of the house to my car.

The van was gone.

I stood staring blankly at the space where I had parked the van with its ignition locked. Here was still another shock to my already dazed mind: my van had completely disappeared.

A small explosion inside of the house—no more than a muffled *blop* reminded me that at any minute the house could blow up; I ducked and ran for cover.

From a copse of trees I looked back: the house still stood, inviolate, its exterior untouched, but from where I'd paused I could see the intense brightness of flames raging behind the windows. When I saw a tongue of flame curl out of one window and lick the clapboards I turned and ran. I had reached the intersection when I heard the scream of the town's fire alarm.

The thunderstorm struck before I had walked a mile, and I had five more miles to go. It didn't occur to me to ask for help or call a taxi; I was officially dead and I knew I had to stay that way. Whoever had tried to kill me had carried away with him the assumption that my charred body wouldn't be found until the firemen sifted the ashes but I thought that he couldn't possibly have followed me to Hannah's house without a car. He would have taken my van to confuse both firemen and police but eventually he would have to come back to retrieve his car from whatever hiding place he'd found, and I didn't intend him to see me, still alive, limping along the highway. I walked at the very edge of the road, and ducked behind a tree whenever I heard a car approaching.

I had been drenched a few seconds after the rain began, but this proved a minor irritant; worse, I had twisted my ankle when I jumped from the porch roof and now it began to throb painfully. I nursed it as well as I could, but most of all I nursed my anger. I had very nearly been dead and I still couldn't adjust to the fact. I mean, how many people get locked into an empty house which is then set on fire? To be the object of so much hostility is difficult for one person to assimilate.

It took me almost two hours to limp to the motel and it was nearly dark when I reached it. My van was parked precisely in front of unit 18. Not in front of 16 or 20, or even the motel office, but squarely in front of number 18.

I had planned a hot bath; I had planned a dinner—after all, we'd eaten nothing but stale peanut butter crackers since breakfast—but finding the van at the motel, in exactly the right place, pushed me beyond reason. I unlocked the back of the van, made certain no one was hiding inside, climbed into the front seat, started the engine, and drove away. I had no idea where I was going; I only knew I was getting away from the Golden Kingfisher Motel, and from Anglesworth, as quickly as possible. I was leaving behind my suitcase with half of my clothes in it, my toothbrush, and an unpaid bill; I was dripping wet, shivering from cold

174

and terror, and my ankle throbbing, but at least I was still alive.

I stopped at a gas station five miles out of Anglesworth and while the tank was filled I noted the few cars that passed. Nobody seemed interested in either the van or me. In the back of the van I found a sweater and my blue jeans; I went into the ladies' room, took off my dripping corduroy suit, rubbed myself dry, and changed into clean clothes. I bought a cup of coffee from the vending machine in the gas station and climbed back into the van. By the time I'd driven fifteen more miles I felt a little safer but utterly wrung out. I stopped at a motel called the Bide-a-Wee that had a restaurant attached to it, and ordered a large dinner which I proceeded to eat because I knew I must. After that I rented a room in the motel, paid in advance, and fell into an exhausted sleep as soon as I dropped across the bed.

When I woke up the rain had stopped and my watch told me it was midnight. By some curious adjustment of time I was now back inside of my own skin again and able to look sanely at what had happened to me during the past few hours. I decided that back there in Hannah's box room, when my mind had tried to rationalize away the shock and my senses had shouted *don't listen,* some kind of split had taken place, blocking off every emotion except what was needed for survival. Now as I emerged from shock I began to feel quite benevolent toward that Amelia; she was all right, she had behaved very soundly. With my mind no longer bruised but able to think again, I could even put aside the idea that a tramp had followed me into the house in Carleton, had playfully locked me into the box room and then set fire to the house. It had been a possibility worth cherishing but I could no longer think why. After all, there was no getting around the fact that Joe and I had come to Maine to look for a murderer, and it was just possible that we had flushed him out. Certainly whoever had followed me into the house had murder on his mind; it was a coincidence that I couldn't afford to overlook.

I tried looking at it now but I wasn't ready for it yet, it only brought a gravelike chill. I walked into the bathroom, ran steaming hot water into the tub and climbed in carrying with me Hannah's manuscript, which was damp from the rain, anyway. Savoring warmth again, and fortified against any new chills, I resumed my reading of *In the Land of the Golden Warriors*.

The story was startling, to say the least.

In the book Colin makes another journey, this time at the request of the Prince of Galt, who has heard of a country far away where the people are wise, their strength great, and their wealth so bountiful that their helmets are lined with gold leaf and shine like the sun. This is the Land of the Golden Warriors. To reach this country Colin must go back through the country he left when he entered the maze at the heart of the castle, a place the Galts call the Old Territory.

Colin sets out alone, but along the way he collects three young people who have been abandoned by the Old Territory people, now grown insulated and selfish. The names of these three young people, scarcely out of their teens, are Rolphe, Jaspar, and Sara, and this is where I began reading with fascination and then horror.

As I watched their characters unfold I read faster and faster, feverishly turning the pages.

Rolphe was thin and serious, with "rusty hair like a squirrel," fascinated by the tales Colin told each night at the camp fire about his earlier journey through the maze. ("Is there really such a country? How I hunger for it!" cries Rolphe.)

Jaspar was at first glance the heroic figure of the three, a handsome lad, and strong, but ever so subtly it emerged that Jaspar was interested in accompanying Colin to the Land of the Golden Warriors only to steal the gold and bring it back.

And Sara...Sara was beautiful and a delight to Colin, grateful for every kindness, but always her eyes remained fixed upon Jaspar. She followed him everywhere, longing to be noticed, competing with him and then submitting to him, trying every means to gain his approval, desperate for a clue to his affections. There was a vivid scene in a forest where they met a witch and Sara begged for a few minutes alone with her. Colin, worried, followed them into the wood and overheard Sara ask the witch for a spell to make Jaspar love her. "Only if you sell me your soul," the witch told her. In horror Colin rushed forward to stop them but a tree root tripped him, and before he could reach Sara, the transaction had taken place: Sara had sold the witch her soul in return for a spell that rendered her and Jaspar inseparable.

The ending was poignant: they had many adventures in the Land of the Golden Warriors but, when the time came to leave, a greedy Jaspar was discovered with gold in his travel bags and he was banished to a prison in that country. Because of the witch's spell Sara was doomed to sit outside that prison, perhaps for an eternity, waiting and waiting, a captive herself. Only Rolphe rode off with Colin; he had chosen to search for the maze in the heart of the castle so that one day he might join Colin in the land of the Galts.

When I had finished reading I sat very still, the steam rising around me in swirls, and then I carefully placed the manuscript out of reach on the floor.

I know that to other people who have read the book by now it is simply a very exciting and beautifully written adventure story with three characters more realistically and compassionately drawn than any of those in her first book. But for me it was a revelation. Hannah was, as Joe had said, no fool: she had insight, and this was her story of three young people whose lives she had shared and observed. If this was Nora when she was young, if this was what Hannah had seen, had she looked ahead to where such obsession could take Nora, and written of it to warn her? Warn her, too, that the boy she loved was equally obsessed, but with gold?

I had tried so hard to be kind as I struggled to explain Nora's presence in the house while Hannah was being killed but she had been an accomplice from the beginning, I knew that now. She must have loved John Tuttle with a passion so unhealthy that it turned into obsession, which allows no choice, is need-gone-wild, displacing morality and judgment, reducing vision and awareness to one exclusive object. When John Tuttle had become important to Nora everyone else had stopped existing for her. He had totally possessed her.

The horror of it rocked me, and yet at the same time I was aware of a compassion for her that I didn't want to admit. A part of me was still back in that forest hearing the witch question Sara, and Sara say, "Jaspar is the sun and the moon and the stars, the mother I never had, the father who never loved me. He is all that I ever want. Make him see me, make him mine."

The mother I never had, the father who never loved me.... The resemblance to my own past was acute. I would have preferred to hate or despise Nora, but at this moment I discovered that I understood and pitied her. If this was wisdom it also frightened me.

I wondered what Hubert Holton's obsession might have been.

I wondered why Jay Tuttle hadn't married Nora once she was rich. I thought of her growing old at Greenacres, I remembered her ravaged face, and I said aloud, fiercely, "Oh Nora, why couldn't you have gotten angry just once at what was being done to you?"

As I was angry now at whoever had tried to kill me in the box room. I still didn't know who, and it was time to find out.

I climbed out of the tub, dressed, tied up Hannah's two hundred pages of story, and resolutely put aside my thoughts of Nora. I knew that of the cozy foursome who had killed Hannah, two were now accounted for but two were distressingly not: John Tuttle and Hubert Holton. I had to assume that it was one of them who had tried to kill me, except that I couldn't puzzle out how they'd learned about Joe and me. Unless Garwin Mason had told one of them. Or Mrs. Morneau.

I thought about this. Mrs. Morneau seemed the more likely candidate except for one important detail: Joe and I had left her house at half-past two that afternoon and we had driven straight to the airport without stopping at unit 18. Considering this, how could I explain the van being returned to the Golden Kingfisher Motel and parked precisely under unit 18? It implied an intelligence that chilled me. It also had the effect of making sleep impossible, because even the most confident of murderers was bound to eventually notice that my van was gone; that would be a shock, and so mystifying that he would feel compelled to find it. What I had to do now was get back to Trafton, and to Joe, but without worrying him, for he at least was safe for the moment. What I also had to do was find John Tuttle but under no circumstances was I going to return to Anglesworth and ask Garwin Mason where he was.

"Ask Nora," Mrs. Morneau had added with a touch of malice.

Very well, I decided, I would ask Nora; there was no harm in that if I could get past Nurse Dawes and persuade Nora to talk. Greenacres was a safe one hundred miles away from Anglesworth and it was on my route back to Trafton. I was fairly sure that Nora would know about Tuttle because I had a hunch that he might be the mysterious friend of the family who paid her bills: I couldn't think who else would. Robin couldn't afford to, nor could Mrs. Morneau, and Nora had spent all her money on a glass house and drink.

I left the motel feeling considerably older, and in a sense I was. For one thing I checked the back of the van again, and opened up the hood to make certain that no one had rearranged any wires. For that matter, if anyone had told me a week ago that I would choose to drive alone at half-past one in the morning I would have collapsed in laughter. It was surprising what a simple equation I had uncovered: when one terror outweighs another, the deeper one will triumph over the lesser.

I had driven ten miles before I realized there was one other person who could have betrayed us to a murderer, and that was Mrs. Daniel Lipton if she had run out of drinking money again.

12

On my long drive down the coast in the middle of the night it seemed as if the most frightening thing about this dark world of greed and conspiracy, of people haunted by a past that relentlessly controlled them, this Hieronymous Bosch landscape that I'd entered—was that it might be reality. It was the old tightrope business again, except that if I glanced down this time I would see not only my mother but Danny Lipton, all bloody from his throat being slashed; Mrs. Morneau stifling her sobs behind a door; Nora lifting herself from her bed to cry over the photograph of a hurdy-gurdy. It was a vision I couldn't bear as I drove those dark, empty roads; it tempted me to give up, but that's what they had all done, and I wanted better company.

Yet there was Joe, and he was reality too. And there was also Amman Singh, and there was Hannah, who had written a book in which the Grand Odlum said, "You must carry the sun inside of you because you will meet with a great and terrifying darkness." Hannah had known all about the tightrope, of this I was sure, but in the photograph her eyes had been serene and unshadowed, except by a smile.

Both Amman Singh and Hannah had found something important.

Or was it, I thought suddenly, that each of them might have *lost* something, some illusion or impertinence that we're taught to regard as legitimately ours but which only keeps us bound hopelessly to a treadmill?

This thought occupied me for the remainder of the drive but I felt the lighter for it.

At half-past three I parked in a rest stop beside the highway, locked myself into the back in my sleeping bag, and slept until dawn filtered through the portholes. After that I drove on to Portland and found an all-night diner where I ate breakfast elbow-to-elbow with truckdrivers and night-shift workers. Obviously something was happening to my safety zones.... At half-past eight I bought a toothbrush and visited Western Union to send Joe a telegram. It was a very difficult one to compose; I wanted to write *I love you, I miss you, I'm scared but I've got to handle this alone so that I know that I can.* The telegram I finally sent was RETURNING HOME, MAY STOP IN NEW YORK TO SEE ROBIN, REACH TRAFTON LATE TOMORROW AFTERNOON HOPE GRISELDA WAS SPARED LOVE AMELIA. I would have preferred to telephone him but I was too much a coward, I was afraid I might say too much and alarm him, or

182

say too little and alarm myself. I felt that a telegram was kinder for both of us: it left out attempted murder, panic, flight, a long night drive, somber thoughts, and breakfast in an all-night diner.

The one thought that never occurred to me was that Joe might have telephoned the Golden Kingfisher Motel during the night to tell me he'd safely reached Trafton. It simply never crossed my conscious mind. This was a symptom, I think, of how I still undervalued myself, and how unaccustomed I was to being tenderly regarded.

In the meantime, at some point during the night I had decided I must deliver Hannah's manuscript to Robin because it belonged to Hannah's heirs, and Robin was certainly the only one to whom I could entrust it. I was also hoping that I might find a tactful way to ask him why he had never appealed that Probate Court decision; I thought I knew the answer but Joe's passion for verifying was infectious.

But first there was Nora to see before I closed the books on this search and turned it over to the police, this Nora who had given everything, including her integrity, to a man who had gone off and left her. I couldn't understand why Jay Tuttle had abandoned her, but every question I asked seemed to lead into a new one. It was like one of those novelty boxes that you open to find a second box neatly fitted inside of it, and then another and another and another. *Why hadn't Tuttle married her?* Nora was beautiful, and heaven only knows she'd been devoted. After the murder she was also rich and, as an accomplice, dangerous to him as well. By every law of logic he should have married her, if only to make sure she would never testify against him, but he hadn't. Why?

This was a good question but unfortunately it exposed another one: Tuttle had gone to enormous

183

lengths to change Hannah's will before she was murdered but if he'd simply killed her and then married Nora without that bogus will he would have married a woman with an inheritance of a million dollars.

It implied that Jay Tuttle had wanted $700,000, but not Nora.

But if this were so there was still another question waiting inside of it: Lipton had been murdered because he was an accomplice. Nora, who was even more involved and more dangerous to them both, had been allowed to survive. Why?

By half-past nine I was circling Greenacres, bumping over the woods roads that surrounded it and keeping my eyes on the rear lawn. I had remembered the nurse saying that Nora would be all right after we left her, and by the next morning would be sitting in the sun in the back with the rest of the patients. By ten o'clock there were a number of people sitting in chairs in the sun, distributed like dolls, each very carefully apart from the other, with a nurse in uniform sitting quietly on the rear porch and reading a book. I parked at the south side of the property and finally saw Nora off to one side, in a white chair with her feet on a hassock. From where I stood it looked as if she was staring into nothingness; the waste of it struck me as appalling.

I slipped through the hedge and walked under the pine trees, their needles soft and pliant under my feet, until I came out on the lawn, which was as soft as a foam rubber carpet. The nurse sitting near the stairs was preoccupied with her book; no heads turned to watch me. I reached Nora and knelt beside her chair.

"Miss Harrington," I said.

She was wearing expensive pale green slacks and a matching pale green blouse that hung on her as if no one had known her size. She wrenched her gaze from

184

some unfathomable dream and frowned at me. It took her eyes a moment to focus. "Yes," she said dully.

"Miss Harrington," I asked, "where can I find John Tuttle?"

This startled her out of her apathy. "He comes here," she faltered, looking surprised. "Sometimes. Once a month I think. He comes to see me." She looked horribly vulnerable, like a child.

"I'd like to know how to reach him," I said gently. "Can you tell me where to find him?"

She peered closer at me, struggling against fog. "Who are you? Did he send you?"

"I'm Amelia Jones, Miss Harrington, and I'm wondering if you can tell me where to find John Tuttle."

"I remember you," she said suddenly. "I've seen you before, you came about the hurdy-gurdy."

"Yes, and I've come back to ask you, please, how to locate Jay Tuttle."

"Jay," she murmured. "Dear Jay. Bastard Jay."

"Yes, but can you tell me where I can find him. Now. Today."

She said sharply, "But he doesn't have anything to do with hurdy-gurdies. You showed me pictures and I cried. You made me cry."

"Yes, you cried when you saw your aunt Hannah's hurdy-gurdy."

"What has that to do with Jay? He doesn't know anything about hurdy-gurdies. It's Robin and I who played with it, it was ours and it was Aunt Hannah's, and we loved it."

"Yes, and you kept it awhile, and then Robin bought it at the auction and kept it awhile, too."

She nodded. "We took turns choosing things and I chose the hurdy-gurdy. I had first choice," she said proudly.

"Yes."

"And that's what I wanted most of all, it was in the box room and I chose it." And then she repeated, "In the box room. . . ." She looked at me and I looked at her and the words hung between us. "The hurdy-gurdy was in the box room," she whispered, and her eyes grew wider and wider as horror and intelligence filled them. "In the same room as. . . ." One hand flew to her mouth. *"Why are you here? Why are you asking me these questions?"*

I said, "Miss Harrington—" But I was too late; she closed her eyes, flung back her head and began screaming.

The young nurse reached her first. She gave me a mute, reproachful glance as she leaned over Nora and then I saw Nurse Dawes running across the lawn to us. "You again!" she shouted. "Out—I'll call the police if you come again, you've no right to sneak in here and harass a patient. What have you done to her? *What have you done to her?"*

"Nothing, I'm going now," I said angrily above Nora's screams. Heads had turned dully toward us in wonder; my eyes held a picture of vivid green lawn and Dr. Ffolks racing toward us in his white jacket, Nora's screams growing sharper and more hysterical. Nurse Dawes was already rolling up Nora's sleeve for still another injection to bring her peace.

"We'll get a court order, Miss Jones—Miss Amelia Jones, isn't it?" shouted Mrs. Dawes over her shoulder. "We're paid to protect our patients."

"I won't bother her again," I said coldly, and I walked away and didn't look back until I'd reached the van. When I turned they were all clustered around Nora, whose screams had turned into sobs now.

I felt a little sick. I climbed into the van and closed my eyes and then I opened them and said "Damn" in a loud voice. I started up the van for my long drive

outh and that, I thought, was that. It was going to
have to be Detective Zebroski after all, unless Robin
knew what had happened to Tuttle, but 1965 was a
long time ago.

I am not one for marathon driving. I stayed the night
in a motel near Westport, Connecticut, and from there
telephoned Robin in New York City. I explained that
was on my way home from Maine, where I'd been
racing the hurdy-gurdy I'd asked him about on the
tairs, and could I see him for a few minutes the next
lay?

He said very politely that he would be at home dur-
ng the morning hours, and then with some amusement
he gave me the directions I asked for on how to approach the city by car. I carefully wrote them down,
eeling an absolute coward about all those parkways
and expressways. I think it's a fear in me of getting
ost; when a person has felt basically lost for half of her
life it is not a situation to be lightly entered or courted.

It was thus with a sense of astonishment and
riumph that I successfully pulled up in front of his
building on East Ninth Street at eleven o'clock the next
norning. It was a sultry day, with the sun hidden behind clouds, and the humidity oppressive; I was still
wearing blue jeans and sweater, so I noticed. I was also
nervous about how much to tell Robin and had tried
out a number of censored versions of how I came to find
Hannah's manuscript in an old mattress.

He must have been watching for me, because no
sooner had I backed into a parking space in front of his
building than he came out of the door and waved at
me. He was wearing faded jeans, a white shirt and
neakers, and again he gave the illusion of great youth
until the light picked out the lines in his face. "Good

morning," he said. "Quite a van, that. I hope you're locking it up from stem to stern."

I felt inexplicably shy as we shook hands; I realized that when I'd last seen him he was a complete stranger, an actor named Robert Lamandale sandwiched between my visit to the colonel and the next day's auction. Now he was Hannah's nephew Robin, someone Hannah had loved, and I knew much more about him. I also knew—it came over me with a sense of rightness—that because of this I was going to tell him the whole story.

I could see that he was puzzled by my being here, and too polite to say so. He turned and led me past the broken intercom and we began the climb to apartment 12. "So you actually went to Maine and visited my cousin," he said over his shoulder.

"Yes," I said, stopping to catch my breath on the third landing. I wanted to ask him if he'd gotten the part he auditioned for on the day I first met him, but I thought it better not to. There was one more landing before he unlocked a door with three locks.

"I've put together some iced tea and peppermint for us," he said. "It's a warm day. I hope my directions worked? No detours, no bad advice?"

"They were perfect," I told him, looking around. It was a one-room apartment, long and narrow, but it was a corner apartment and with the building on its flank gone it was full of light. There was a shabby kitchenette on my right, with a stained refrigerator and an ancient gas stove, but the other end was very different: the white walls held a line of well-framed theatrical photographs over the low couch, there was a low square table with one flower in a vase, three square cushions on the floor, and a wall of bookcases built out of lumber and bricks; the result was a feeling of space carved out of smallness. I walked over to the bookcase and saw that one shelf was filled with books on Zen: van de

Wetering, Humphreys, both Suzukis, Lama Yongdan, Evans-Wertz, Herrigel. "I see you're interested in Zen," I called over my shoulder.

"An aunt of mine was," he said almost curtly, dropping ice cubes into two tall glasses. "Shall we sit here?" he suggested, carrying the glasses to the shabby chrome-and-plastic dining table.

"Your aunt Hannah Gruble," I said deliberately, "who wrote *The Maze in the Heart of the Castle*."

He stopped short, the glasses still in his hand. He said quietly, "I think you'd better tell me what this is all about, don't you? It was a hurdy-gurdy you were tracing last week. Or so you said."

"It *was* a hurdy-gurdy," I told him, "but I was tracing it because of a note I found inside it, a note signed with the name Hannah. Just Hannah. No last name."

He looked baffled. "A note inside a hurdy-gurdy?"

"Your aunt originally owned it, didn't she?"

"Yes she did, but she wasn't the sort of person to—" He stopped, frowning. "May I ask what on earth the note said to inspire such curiosity on your part?"

I hesitated, wanting to ease into this gently. "It suggested that an accident was being arranged for her, and that she was going to die soon."

"But that's preposterous," he said. "It's absolutely ridic—" He bit off his words, abruptly turned away and walked over to the window where he stood with his back to me. There was a long silence; when he turned to face me again he looked shaken. "I'm sorry, that was a stupid thing to say."

"Because it doesn't entirely surprise you?"

He returned to the table. "Shall we sit down?" he said wryly. "I take it that you've been doing a bit of research into my family."

I nodded. "You're Robin, for instance, Robin Gruble. And your cousin is Nora."

"That matters?"

"The names were in the note," I said. "Robin and Nora." I began digging in my purse for Hannah's note. "My friend Joe Osbourne was in Maine with me until he had to fly home. We visited Nora, and we visited your aunt's house in Carleton, her attorney Garwin Mason, and your aunt's housekeeper Mrs. Morneau."

"All those people?" He looked startled. "I've never cared to go back, you know. I've not set foot in Anglesworth or Carleton since 1965. I've done summer stock in the playhouses but I've always avoided Anglesworth."

I brought out the note and said, "Mr. Lamandale, could I ask you why you went to all the trouble and expense of a Probate Court hearing on your aunt's will and then didn't appeal the verdict, or carry it to the higher court? Why did you give up?"

He whistled soundlessly through his teeth. "You really go for the jugular, don't you."

"Why?" I repeated.

"And why should I tell you?" he asked calmly.

"Was it because of Nora?"

He shrugged and lifted his glass of tea. "Cheers," he said and then, "Look, I'm sorry but I don't know a blasted thing about you. You stop in here on a cloudy May morning and out of the blue you tell me, or suggest—"

"Here's a photostat of the note," I told him, and handed it across the table.

As soon as Robin saw the handwriting he looked shaken. "Oh my God," he whispered, and when he'd finished reading it he carefully placed it on the table, his face white. "This was inside the hurdy-gurdy?"

I nodded. "The hurdy-gurdy came with my shop, the Ebbtide Shop in Trafton, when I bought out Mr. Georgerakis. I kept the hurdy-gurdy for myself, and then one night it wouldn't play. This piece of paper had caught in the mechanism."

"And because of this—" I could see he was concentrating on me while he struggled to face the contents of the note. "Because of this you've taken time out of your life to learn who wrote it? I find that—I don't know whether to say astonishing or touching or—"

I said dryly, "You could, if you like, think of Joe and me as simply avenging angels or demons: Jones and Osbourne, witch and warlock, stirring up messy brews with a teaspoon." I didn't want to tell him how messy it had grown at the end, I preferred to wipe away the stricken look on his face. I brought out the manila folder I'd purchased in Westport, removed the pages of the manuscript and pushed them across the table to him. "There's this, too," I said gently. "Exhibit B, as proof of my sincerity. In exchange for information I'd like very much to have."

"Hannah's book," he said, staring at it incredulously. "Hannah's *book*?" He added abruptly, "Look, do you mind if I have a drink of something stronger? You're throwing shock after shock at me. I've only one shot of brandy left or I'd—"

"Go right ahead," I urged. "I think you need it."

He nodded, reached into a cupboard and emptied a bottle of brandy into a shot glass. He brought it back to the table and sat down, staring at it, not touching it yet. "You've brought back a very old nightmare," he said slowly, "and one that I'm not sure I feel like talking about yet. But I can at the very least answer your questions, I owe you that if only for the miracle of your finding Hannah's manuscript."

"You knew of its existence?"

He nodded. "She told me about it when I visited her the Easter before her death. She said once it was typed up she'd Xerox a copy and send it to me." He hesitated and then he added quietly, "I think you asked about the will."

"Yes," I said, watching him.

"I never quite believed in it, no. I find that people are creatures of habit and custom," he said, "and Hannah was no exception. She'd always very scrupulously sent copies to us, you know—whenever she made changes in her will—and they were always drawn up for her by Garwin Mason, who was a good friend of hers. And then she went against habit and custom, typed up a will by herself, and her death happened so *very* soon afterward. . . ."

He picked up the shot glass, tossed its contents down his throat and made a face. "But everywhere I turned," he said, lifting his eyes to meet mine, "there was Nora."

I nodded. "And everywhere *we* turned there was Nora. Is that why you didn't appeal the verdict?"

"Of course," he said simply.

I waited; the brandy was having its effect and the color was returning to his face. "Garwin Mason warned me," he went on. "Warned me that accusing Jay Tuttle of undue influence would fail—had to fail—because I wasn't prepared to go far enough. Do you know what the legal definition of 'undue influence' is in Maine?"

I shook my head.

"I memorized it," he said, and closing his eyes recited, "'. . . amounting to moral coercion, destroying free agency, or importunity which could not be resisted, so that the testator, unable to withstand the influence, or too weak to resist it, was constrained to do that which was not his actual will but against it.'" He opened his eyes. "How could I accuse Nora of coercion? I went ahead with the hearing because I thought some piece of testimony given under oath might explain away my uneasiness. I hoped against hope the hearing would explain the inexplicable, but it turned up nothing except the increasing suspicion that pursuing the matter further could destroy Nora."

I said without thinking, "It destroyed her anyway, didn't it?"

He said with a sigh, "How was one to know? You can't possibly realize how it was with us, or what Nora was like when we were growing up together. We were like brother and sister for each summer of the year, living in a magic world that Aunt Hannah created for us. If you'd ever read her book—"

I didn't interrupt.

"—you'd know Hannah's inventiveness, the wealth of her imagination. She applied that to living, too. There were picnics, treasure hunts, acting out plays on the sunporch, long evenings reading aloud to each other in front of the fire. Absurd games. A trip to the river every sunny afternoon with an incredible paraphernalia of swimming things, tubes, water wings, robes, and always Aunt Hannah's Tibetan parasol...."

"It sounds—lovely," I said with a catch in my voice.

"But afterward," he went on, his voice tightening, "Nora would go home to a cold father and an impossible stepmother, both of whom argued tirelessly over money and gave evidence of disliking Nora very much, and I would go back to my father who, following my mother's death, packed me off to private schools or camps as hastily as possible. Which, by the way, I've no doubt that Aunt Hannah paid for. During those endless dismal months of reality we exchanged letters: Aunt Hannah's tranquil and supportive, Nora's desperate, and mine lonely.

"We were, you see, very close," he concluded, and then he added, "at least until Nora fell in love."

Ah, yes, I thought, now we come to it, and I could feel my pulses quickening. "With Jay Tuttle."

"You guessed, then?"

I said, "I have the advantage of you, I read your aunt's manuscript last night. You'll understand what I mean when you've read it, too. Until then I'd hoped she was blackmailed."

His smile was bleak. "I wonder if one can exclude blackmail in an unholy kind of love like Nora's." He shook his head. "It must always have been there but I never saw. Hannah did, because I remember one day when Nora was only eleven or twelve years old, we were down by the river and I saw Aunt Hannah watching her with a very sad expression. I asked her what was wrong and she said, 'Robin, I want you to promise to be very patient with Nora, and very wise. There's an emptiness inside of her, a desperate need to be loved, and there's nothing you or I can do but try and protect her.' I didn't know what she was talking about then, but only a few years later the words came back to haunt me. From the moment that Nora met Jay—she was fourteen, I think—no one else existed for her. She dumped everything she was or could be into his lap."

"Compulsion?"

"Compulsion, obsession, emotional deprivation—" He shrugged. "Whatever you choose to call it. She was so lovely, like a fairy-tale princess. I have snapshots somewhere, I'll show you in a moment." He got up and began rummaging in a desk drawer. "She could have had anyone, but Jay arrived first and that was that."

"Did he seem to care for her too?"

"It was always difficult to know what Jay was thinking or feeling, he was always so bloody charming." He came back with a large, bulging envelope. "Certainly he was very attentive the last time I saw them together. At Easter, that was, when Hannah told me—in confidence—about her new book. Several weeks after that Nora phoned me in New York one night, terribly excited, to say that she and Jay were going to be married in the fall."

"Married," I repeated, calculating dates very cynically. In the fall . . . after she had lent her help to a murder.

"Which led," he added bitterly, "to my final rationalization: it occurred to me after her death that Hannah *could* have changed her will on impulse if she felt that it would make Jay and Nora 'equal' enough to marry."

"That could always have been possible," I told him for comfort.

He laughed bleakly. "It seemed so to me, too, even though it was completely uncharacteristic of Hannah. But of course the only other possibility was too godawful to contemplate: that Nora had been just unstable enough, besotted enough—" He shivered. "She adored Hannah, which makes it so—so—"

"They never married," I pointed out.

"No."

"Do you know why?"

"I never asked," he said. "I remained stubbornly in New York, sinking my inheritance into plays that only proved what poor judgment I had, and nursing a dazzling career that shot down as fast as it had shot up. If I considered Nora's situation at all I'm sure I told myself that Aunt Hannah would never have wanted to see Nora destroyed. Not that I ever considered it consciously," he explained. "I shoved it under, burying my nagging little doubts." He looked at me steadily and took a deep breath. "All right," he said. "What do you believe happened? I think I can take it now."

And so I told him. His aunt a captive. The long days and nights in the box room where I'd found her manuscript. The signing of the will at last, and then being taken out of the box room and led downstairs.

"God," said Robin, going white again. "And then?"

"It's only a theory but I think she must have been blindfolded," I told him. "I think they confused her sense of direction, hurried her along the hall toward the kitchen with the cellar door ahead wide open at the end of that long hall—"

"Yes, I know that hall," he said, nodding.

"—and when she reached the threshold of the doorway they pushed her. It was the only way to do it—by trickery—that would leave no marks."

"Who?" demanded Robin.

"John Tuttle and Holton . . . I think with the help of Daniel Lipton, whose throat was cut five months later."

"I didn't know him," Robin said. "You're leaving out Nora, aren't you?"

"I think the last two—Holton and Lipton—were the 'faceless ones.'" Seeing how awful Robin looked I added politely, "It's really possible, you know, that Nora tried to break away at the end, that she couldn't face what was happening. She left for those two days, you know."

"Kind of you," he said with a twisted smile, "but she came back, didn't she? How was she when you saw her at the hospital?"

I thought about this. "Like someone who had died a long time ago," I said quietly, "leaving only a shell behind."

"I wish I could hate her," he said. He reached into the envelope, sorted through a few snapshots and handed one to me. "Here's the Nora I knew and loved."

She was sitting in a hammock, probably no older than fourteen, wearing grubby pants and a torn shirt that somehow made her beauty all the more potent. I felt a pang of envy—that long blond hair, the eager, radiant face, the flawless features. She was lovelier than anyone I'd ever seen; a fairy-tale princess indeed. "Who's the boy behind her?" I asked as my eyes moved away from her face. I frowned. It's not you, it can't be, yet he looks so familiar to me."

Robin leaned over and looked. "Oh. That's Jay Tuttle."

"We have yet to find him," I told Robin. "I don't suppose you've kept track of him at all, have you?"

He looked at me strangely. "You mean you don't know?"

My frown deepened. "Well, you see, Nora wouldn't tell me yesterday, and Mrs. Morneau seemed too—too frightened to tell us. She said he'd changed his name, changed a good many other things, too. She refused to tell us where to find him, and under what name."

Robin's laugh was harsh. "Morney was never one to go against the Establishment, no." Getting up he walked over to his bookcase and baffled me by returning with a recent copy of *Newsweek* magazine. "Here," he said, turning the pages. "Under 'New Crop of Candidates.' They're arranged alphabetically according to states. Look under Maine."

But of course as soon as he spoke the word "candidate," the truth struck me. Nevertheless I leaned over the page and searched for the pictures of the two men who were running against the incumbent in Maine for the U. S. Senate. And there they were: *Angus Tuttle* and *Silas Whitney*.

"Morney was misleading you," Robin said. "Jay changed only his first name. Catchier, making it Angus. The plainness of his name always irritated him but believe me, he would *never* consider changing the Tuttle, it brought him too many votes in Maine. If you'd known him you'd have realized *that*."

He pointed at the toothpaste-ad smile that had bedecked the telephone poles, the restaurant mirrors and the general stores of Anglesworth and Carleton. "There's your John Tuttle," he said, "and Holton is his aide."

197

I said stupidly, "There are twelve teeth in that smile," but my stomach had tightened. Dear God, I was thinking, what have I gotten us into, no one on earth is going to believe this man is a murderer.

13

It was raining when I left New York City, a slanting, silvery rain that was already cooling the air. I had telephoned Joe from Robin's apartment to tell him about Tuttle but there had been no answer; all I could think about now was getting back to Trafton and seeing him. I think I was channeling all of my shock into picturing Joe's; without this anticipation I would have had to face the anxiety I was experiencing. After all, Woodward had Bernstein, and Bernstein had Woodward.

What worsened the sense of shock was that I'd honestly never given a thought to what Tuttle might have become, I'd been concentrating exclusively on Hannah. Perhaps because my mother had inculcated such heavy guilts in me as a child I had assumed that Tuttle would be living defensively, as I would, given to trembling atthe sight of every policeman, with the occasional nightmare from which he awoke drenched with sweat.

Now I realized how unimaginative I'd been.

A murderer, I realized, must first of all have a great and consuming ego, something like an overgrown and poisonous mushroom I decided as I pictured it, even compared it, to my own ego, which I had often felt must resemble a withered prune. There would have to be something missing inside a murderer, a sense of connectedness to other people, so that he would see them as satellites to feed and nourish him, not as human beings just like himself. The thought of any similarity between himself and others would be intolerable, he would be cleverer, more resourceful, realistic and intelligent, and after he had successfully murdered he would think of himself as God, wouldn't he?

Obviously I had overlooked the conceit and the arrogance. He wouldn't tremble at the sight of a policeman, he would smile, his secret glowing inside of him, his superiority reinforced.

As to what to do about Tuttle, Joe would know, Joe would know exactly what to do and which people to see, as Robin had not. "I'm an actor," Robin had explained. "With Hannah's manuscript I'm on familiar, solid ground, you can trust me there. I know the agent she had, and I know the agent's going to be excited as hell about this sequel. All this I can handle, it's part of my scene. Murder, no."

Of course I had not told him about Hannah's house burning down, with me very nearly trapped inside, but that had happened in Maine. Now I was leaving New York and heading for Pennsylvania, and Maine felt a long time ago, distinctly unreal and very far away.

I entered Trafton feeling that, given any encouragement, I would jump out of the van and kiss its pavements. It was just six o'clock as I drove down the boulevard, turned up Grand Street, and then down Cherry so that I would come out on the 900 block of Fleet Street. I had been absent for six days; during that time Trafton had acquired a patina and a charm I'd never before noticed. I slid the van skillfully into a parking slot in front of Joe's office, slipped a dime into the parking meter, and raced upstairs to his door.

The first thing I saw was my telegram lying on the floor mat. Unopened.

This was certainly jarring. I'd sent this telegram yesterday morning, on Wednesday, and this was early Thursday evening. I couldn't imagine why it was lying there carelessly on the mat some thirty-four hours later. I rattled the door and then banged on it because there was always the possibility that Joe's phone had been out of order for days and the telegram had just been delivered, but I was only playing for time while my heart adjusted to disappointment. I'd nobly overlooked Joe's not waiting for me on the steps outside, I'd forgiven his not seeing me from his window and rushing down to greet me but Joe hadn't even known I was coming; the let-down was considerable. Like Mrs. Morneau I'd been writing scenarios ever since I left New York City; I'd expected to be crushed in a passionate embrace, told I'd been missed (savagely) and the dialogue, while scarcely immortal, had contained only a few clichés and had flirted here and there with R ratings.

All right, I thought grimly, *this is the way life is, Amelia.*

I climbed back into the van and headed north to my own block of Fleet Street. The shop would have closed at six but I could telephone Mr. Georgerakis and tell him of my return, and I was sure he would have a number of anecdotes as well as a warm welcome for me. This revived me. I reminded myself that Joe would eventually come home—after all, he lived here—and I could picture his chagrin when he found my two-day-old telegram on his doorstep. I was suddenly anxious to see my shop now, and Pegasus and the hurdy-gurdy.

I parked the van in the alley, fumbled for my keys and unlocked the door of number 688. The shop looked cheerful and tidy. I hurried upstairs to check my plants and found that Mr. Georgerakis had watered them, just as he'd promised. I came downstairs and looked around with satisfaction, noting that three more bathrobes had been sold, two clocks, and quite a few pieces of the willow ware. To round out this satisfying moment someone began knocking on the shop door and my heart lifted as I realized that it could only be Joe. I eagerly unlocked the door and opened it.

It wasn't Joe. It was a well-dressed, gray-haired man carrying an attaché case.

"I *am* sorry," he said, noticing my disappointment, "but I'm frankly glad you haven't left yet, I was to pick up a case of willow ware? I was here earlier, as perhaps the gentleman told you, the one who was in the shop this afternoon."

"He didn't tell me. A whole case?" I repeated, charmed by the thought in spite of my second disappointment.

"An eight-place setting."

This was very nice indeed: not many people in my neighborhood can afford even a four-place setting all at once, they buy a dish or two at a time. An eight-place setting came to thirty-five dollars, of which my profit was seven-fifty. "Come in by all means," I told him, opening the door wider.

He nodded and walked inside. I knew I'd seen him before and I wondered if he worked in the neighborhood and passed the shop frequently. The most conspicuous feature about him was his glasses, which were round

202

steel-rimmed, and very large; and his clothes, which were conservative and well cut, with a gleam of gold at the wrist. Otherwise he was literally colorless, with that parchment-pale skin that older men have who rarely see the sun, a pair of thin lips, and a short, fleshy nose. But somewhere I'd seen him before. "I'll be only a minute," I told him. "I'll just open up the case and make sure there's been no breakage." I added anxiously, "You do realize it will be thirty-five dollars plus tax?" As soon as I said this I realized how stupid I sounded; he looked like a man who could afford antique willow ware or Limoges or expensive hand-crafted pottery. I deserved the faintly amused look he gave me as he reassured me that he did indeed know the price.

I hauled the case out from under the rear shelves, reached for the stubby penknife hanging from its hook and knelt beside the case. As I slit open the top of the carton I suddenly realized that I'd not seen this man on Fleet Street.

I didn't think I'd seen him in Trafton, either.

I associated that face—those large round glasses and the attaché case—with a background of wooden benches.

This was puzzling: wooden benches. I closed my eyes and hoped that something else would swim to the surface. Wooden benches. A feeling of haste and sadness, too. A face noticed. Other faces. And wooden benches.

I'd been alone. Or had I?

I bent over the dishes, my fingers exploring the china. "Nothing broken," I called cheerfully over my shoulder, and tucked the ends of the carton back in place. "She's all yours," I added.

Where had I encountered wooden benches lately, and why was I so sure that it had been lately? And then I thought, *It had something to do with Joe. Joe was with me.*

I picked up the case and half turned to look at the

man again. He didn't see me. He had quietly walked over to the door where he was clearly outlined against the white shade that I pull down every evening, with CLOSED printed on the street side. Now I saw him reach out and touch the lock, and as I heard it quietly snap—with that crazy *ping!* sound they make—I caught my breath. There had been wooden benches at the Blue Harbor airport in Maine, and that was where I'd seen him; he'd followed us into the waiting room looking conspicuously out of place with his attaché case, conservative business suit and large steel-rimmed glasses. I'd watched him with amusement and after that, I remembered, I'd kissed Joe goodby, driven back to unit 18 and then to Hannah's house and the box room, after which ... but here my thought stopped. My heart almost did, too; it was the sound of the lock that did it. Once before I'd heard a lock snap unexpectedly, in Hannah's box room, and now I had the suffocating feeling that I had just met the person who had turned that lock, too.

I didn't hang up the penknife on its hook; I slipped it instead into my pocket.

Amelia, I thought, *remain calm.*

Amelia, I told myself sharply, *don't panic, the life you save could be your own.*

Except he wouldn't dare to try anything here, whoever he was, surely not in the middle of a city, on a busy street. . . .

Oh no? sneered a part of my mind. *He's just locked the door, hasn't he? The two of you are quite alone and no one in Trafton knows you're back. He wouldn't find a better chance in a million years, would he?*

The telephone, I thought, *somehow I've got to get to the telephone.*

I pretended that I'd neither seen nor heard him lock the door. I strolled toward the counter and toward the

elephone behind it with a bright false smile on my
ace and the case of dishes in front of me like a shield.
As I neared the counter I saw his attaché case lying
here and I saw the letters stamped on it in gold: H.
Holton.

Hubert Holton. I had a nearly overwhelming urge
o scream but I took my hysteria and shoved it deep
nside of me—it was like stuffing something away in
a dufflebag—where I could feel it turning in the pit of
my stomach but fueling me in a more disciplined way.
I said calmly, "I believe Mr. Georgerakis still has these
dishes on sale at 20 per cent off. I'll just give him a ring
and ask—"

"No," he said with equal calm. "I've no time for that."

I lifted the case and threw it at him across the six
or seven feet that separated us but there was nothing
slow about his reflexes, he ducked and the case hit the
floor with a thud and a crash of broken china. Before
I could reach the telephone he picked up the long scissors lying across the dry goods and cut the telephone
wire. Following this he brought a small, businesslike
gun out of his pocket and leveled it at me.

"All right," he said evenly, "how did you know?"

"I noticed you in Maine, at the Blue Harbor airport,"
I told him.

He nodded. "Quite a remarkable young woman."

So I was remarkable; that was pleasant to hear but
not from him. "And you're Hubert Holton."

"You're also a trouble-maker," he pointed out in his
soft, precise, emotionless voice, "and I don't appreciate
trouble-makers."

"No," I said, watching him, "two murders *can* be
embarrassing." I shouldn't have said that, of course,
because until that moment I don't suppose he was
aware of how much I knew, but I wanted to fling much
more than a case of dishes in his face.

205

He blinked at that, and his voice sharpened. "What led you to Anglesworth? I've checked, and so far as I can discover you never knew Hannah Meerloo, or Jay, or Nora. What prompted this idiotic excursion of yours into the past?"

I countered, "First tell me how you heard I was making that excursion."

He shrugged. "Mrs. Lipton phoned me—I was in Augusta—and told me that you and a young man, driving a very distinctive van, had visited her to ask about Danny's witnessing Mrs. Meerloo's will in 1965. She thought it might be worth a few dollars to her. I thought it worth attending to personally, and with not many motels open yet I soon found your van parked at the Golden Kingfisher Motel, and of course the name of your shop here was on the side of the van. After that I followed you to Mrs. Morneau's house and then to the airport, and then—" He stopped and added harshly, "And Jay had a hysterical phone call yesterday from Nora telling him about your visit."

"You mean telling you that I'd survived," I said softly. "You left out your attempt to kill me in Carleton, Mr. Holton."

"So I did," he said smoothly. "As I say, a quite remarkable young woman, and now I'd like to hear what took you to Maine in the first place."

I shook my head. "I don't think so, Mr. Holton, because I don't like people who try to kill me and I'd prefer to let you always wonder how I knew about Hannah. You goofed, you know."

"I do not," he said coldly, "'goof,' as you phrase it." He looked at me as if he were assessing a balance sheet, weighing deficiencies and possibilities. "What you fail to understand, my dear Miss Jones," he said, as if delivering a lecture to a class of backward students, "is that not even the police would be interested in such ancient deaths. I think you've forgotten—if you ever knew—that there's such a thing as a statute of limiations."

"Oh?" I said. I hoped it wasn't true. I refused to believe it was true. "Then why are you so—uh—upset?"

"Because your nuisance value is considerable," he pointed out, "and I simply cannot allow you to jeopardize Jay's chances of being elected to the U. S. Senate. I've worked too hard."

"*You've* worked too hard?" His eyes were like cold gray marbles behind his glasses but his manner was calm; it was difficult to realize that although we were skirting the issue we were really talking about my death.

"Of course," he said, surprised by my obtuseness. "I waited a long, long time to find Jay, and I've taught him everything he knows. He's young, he's only beginning, there's no limit to how far he can go in politics."

I stared at him. "You killed Hannah for *that*?" I said incredulously. "A woman with more talent, imagination and intelligence than that precious Tuttle of yours could ever have?"

He shrugged off my naïveté as if it were a mosquito: impatiently. "She was only a woman," he said contemptuously. "And you show a tiresome interest in the past that doesn't become a person of your age," he added, "For myself it's the future that matters, not the past past."

I blurted out, "Why didn't Jay marry Nora?"

I swear that he looked shocked by my question. "*Marry?*" he repeated. "But my dear Miss Jones I had no intention of letting him marry Nora, it was money he needed, a grubstake one might say. He didn't have a dime, and I had only a professor's modest salary. Jay needed money for clothes, meeting the right people, for entree into the cliques that matter."

I must have looked just as shocked as he had looked a moment ago. I said, "But Nora had money, and Nora loved him."

He smiled forgivingly. "One does not sell a personality like Jay Tuttle's so cheaply, Miss Jones. Nora's inheritance, once taxes were paid, was not so large as you might assume. With money of his own Jay could do much better, and he did. Before the year ended I was happy to see him safely married to Senator Plumtree's daughter Janet, and I can assure you that an heiress to the Plumtree Pharmaceutical fortune, and the prospects of a father-in-law in Washington, made Nora look very small-league and provincial."

I simply gaped at him, wordless, and then I gasped, "You arranged it!"

"But of course," he said silkily. "The Plumtrees had always summered in Maine, and I made a point of meeting them in 1964."

"My God," I whispered, and then I flung at him bitterly, "I'm surprised you let Nora go on living with all she knew about you both."

His lips tightened. "Only at Jay's insistence," he said. "The one time he—but it has always been a mistake, and it's not one I plan to repeat now, Miss Jones. You will be shot beside your cash register—"

He means I'm really going to be killed, I thought. *Me.*

He made a soft tch-tch sound in his throat. "A pity, that. You can see what a nuisance you're proving to me, but I appreciate your telling me this." He gave me his first real smile; his teeth were expensive, too. "A few more deaths will scarcely be noticed among all the muggings and robberies these days but it does seem a bore. Kindly move to the cash register now."

"Kindly?" I echoed, and I laughed, I couldn't help it. I mean, he was going to kill all of us and it seemed a bore? "*Kindly* move to the cash register?" I repeated.

He gave me an impatient glance and I saw that I was reacting like a human being and this was tiresome to a man who thought and performed like a machine, like a computer that turns people into figures on a balance sheet. I think it was this that shocked me even more than his announcing that I was going to be shot beside the cash register, for it's compassion that makes gods of us.

He gestured with his gun. "Over," he said, and when I didn't move he came to get me.

He could have shot me from where he stood but he was obviously a perfectionist, wanting things precisely right for the police. His computer mind must have written its own kind of scenario, planning distance and powder burns, and this rigidness was his first mistake because I was waiting for him with my fingers curled around the penknife, my anger as cold as steel now. Just as he reached for my arm I lifted the penknife out of my pocket and plunged it into his gleaming white shirt. It was a small knife, scarcely an inch in length, but his reaction gave me two seconds to get away. He yelped in pain.

I knew I wouldn't have a chance if I ran for the street door, I'd be shot before I unbolted the lock. I headed instead for the stairs; one bullet hit the wall behind me as I raced up them two at a time. I passed the door to my apartment, opened the one leading to the roof, closed it behind me and ran up the narrow stairs, unbolted the steel door at the top and plunged out on the flat graveled roof of my building.

It was a shock to discover that it was almost dark. I didn't pause. I raced across the gravel, dodging chimneys and apertures, and pulled myself up to the neighboring roof, three feet higher, where I checked the steel door leading down into this building: locked, of course. Over my shoulder I saw Holton's head silhouetted against the sky as he climbed over the parapet behind me. I turned and jumped down to the next roof and stopped to examine the trap door here. No luck. I ran toward the edge of the third roof and abruptly came to a halt. I was facing an alleyway wide enough to park a car and too broad to jump. My escape was blocked. I was trapped.

Fifty feet below me traffic passed in a steady stream; I shouted but no one heard. I turned and saw Holton scrambling down from the roof I'd just left and I could feel my adrenalin glands pouring out fight-or-flight screams, and my heart thudding mercilessly. There were two broken pieces of brick lying near me; I picked them up and hurled one at the empty window across the alley. The sound of breaking glass was muted, no more than a small whimper in the night—or was it I who whimpered?—but no one came to the window.

I turned, grasping the one fragment of brick left me, and faced this man who had already killed twice.

He was walking toward me slowly, still breathing heavily from the climb but he was confident now and smiling faintly in the dusk, the gun in his hand pointed at me. I had two choices: I could climb over the parapet and leap to my death on the street fifty feet below me or I could stand here and be killed on the roof by Hubert Holton. In that moment I looked clearly and sanely into death and I was no longer afraid, I was angry.

I began walking forward to meet him and then abruptly I ducked my head and ran, weaving and zig-zagging. The first bullet hit and staggered me; my left arm felt as if it had been torn away but it had the effect of shocking me into a deeper fury. The second bullet grazed my temple, or so I thought until blood streamed into my eyes, but by that time I was under his gun and on Holton, kicking, screaming, biting. I had no thought for myself any more, only for this man who had the

210

effrontery to kill—kill Hannah, kill Lipton, and now me. My left arm was dead but my right hand could still grasp my shard of brick, my knees could still kick. In the darkness we began a silent fight for the gun; when my teeth found his wrist the gun dropped to the roof, I kicked it aside and hit him with the brick and this time, caught off balance, he fell.

I leaned over him, and seeing how still he was I straightened up, gasping at the agony of being upright, and at the pain in my head. I was crying now with huge, dry, soundless sobs. Dragging myself across the roof I managed to pull my body weakly over the parapet to the next building. I crept across it and half fell, half jumped to the roof of my own building. Here I nearly passed out but I pushed myself to the door, which Holton had left open. For just a moment here I leaned against a wall, sucking in air with great gulps, giddy and nearly blinded from the blood streaming into my eyes, and then I sat down on the stairs and lowered myself, step by step, still sitting—I could never have stood—until I reached the second floor and the stairs leading down to the shop.

That was when I stopped to wipe the blood from my eyes and saw him.

He was standing at the bottom of the stairs watching me. Watching me from the first floor, from a pool of light in the shop. I should have known he'd be here, too. I stared down at him through a film of blood, recognizing him from his pictures except that he wasn't smiling now, those flawless twelve teeth were hidden. John Tuttle . . . State Senator Angus Tuttle now. He looked pale, strained, appalled at the sight of me. I saw him stare at me and lick his lips.

"You're supposed to be dead," he whispered. It was a whisper that seemed to echo through a hundred caverns, reverberating and ricocheting off the walls.

211

I shouted at him, "You can't even do your own killing," and, still crawling, I reached the top stair and looked down at him a second time.

He had brought a pistol from his overcoat pocket and was staring at it in surprise. He lifted his eyes to look at me and licked his lips again. "Where's Hubert?" he asked, and then he shouted, "Hubert, where are you? Hu, for God's sake finish her off!"

I wasn't thinking any longer, I was a bloody wounded dying animal without reaction or fear. He was going to shoot me and finish the job and it no longer mattered, all that mattered was to die as quickly and as obtrusively as possible, and with dignity. For this I was ready to give away my life, and freely. I felt for the railing and pulled myself to my feet, my head exploding like a balloon, the walls circling around me, the stairs swaying in front of me. But I stood. It was going to have to be an execution, a real murder this time, not hidden and concealed for years and years.

Behind me I heard Holton shout from the top of the stairs and below me I saw Tuttle lift his pistol. I stood erect and gritted my teeth, a great dizziness sweeping over me until abruptly the dizziness was joined with darkness and I fell just as a gun exploded, fell endlessly, the roar of blood in my ears, until I came to rest on something soft. Dimly I heard a crash of splintering glass, and voices shouting. Opening my eyes I stared into one sightless, unblinking eye scarcely an inch away from me, an eye that receded, swam closer and then receded until at last, hearing Joe's voice among the others, I gave myself up to the voluptuous, fathomless oblivion of unconsciousness.

PART III

"Do you mean I can never go back?" asked
Colin. . . . "No," said the Prince of Galt, "for
you have gone through the maze."

from *The Maze in the Heart of the
Castle*

14

It was a long journey, full of darkness at first, and whispering voices I knew I'd heard before but couldn't identify. And it was cold, a glacial cold that numbed and paralyzed. As my perceptions sharpened I realized that I was in a labyrinth, with walls binding me on either side, and it was the faint sound of music that drew me forward. I walked on, turning corner after corner, sometimes seeing faint shapes in front of me that turned into mist when I reached them. Yet someone was with me, I knew this; someone I could neither see nor touch but whose presence was familiar, peaceful and very close: I was not entirely alone. The maze twisted and turned and I stumbled on, subtly guided by this presence until suddenly I felt intimations of warmth ahead, and turning into a long passageway I saw light, and began to run, and as I ran I saw that I was leaving behind pieces of myself, like outgrown clothing, until I felt transparent, weightless and at last without fear.

Reluctantly I opened my eyes. A lighted room. White walls. A young man with black hair sitting in a red Naugahyde chair reading a magazine. The two worlds converged, split apart, the labyrinth receding before certain images of pain and violence, a rooftop and a gun. I was not dead, I was lying in a bed, all white and pristine, the blood wiped away from my eyes, my left arm in a splint; I felt incredibly tidy. I was alive and it was Joe sitting in the leather chair. I said softly, tentatively, "Joe."

"Amelia?" He jumped up and came to my bed. "My God, Amelia, welcome back."

"Yes," I said, smiling at him mistily.

He said in a funny kind of voice that shook a little, "I love you, Amelia. Quite awfully, as a matter of fact."

"You understand," I said carefully and slowly, "I'm surprised."

"At my loving you?" He sounded startled.

"No," I said, thinking about this, "at being alive." I turned this slowly over in my mind, and frowned. "There was an eye.... Why do I keep remembering an eye, Joe?"

Joe must have understood that I wasn't functioning yet at his level because he said gently, "Possibly because you landed on top of Jay Tuttle when you fell down the stairs, Amelia."

"I did that, too?" I said, marveling.

"You were damn lucky, actually. As the police put it all together," he explained, "Holton shot you from behind, from the top of the stairs, and at that same

216

exactly what I'd thought it meant: capable of submission to test, readily brought to yield or to submit. Unamenable Amelia, I thought with grim humor, and lay in bed staring at the ceiling and hearing my mother saying from her grave, "You see?"

That did it. The next day, Friday, I arose sane, if grief can be called a form of insanity. Joe had come and Joe had gone: never mind, the sun had still risen, I was twenty-two and I had promises to keep. To Hannah. Mr. Georgerakis stopped in at noon to be shown where everything was, and he displayed his usual deadpan self.

"Miss Jones, I worry about you," he said. "This is the Ebbtide Shop, or maybe Macy's?"

"Ebbtide," I said, playing straight man as usual.

"I would never have known." He shook his head. "Watch your profits, Miss Jones, in this business it's in pennies, not dollars. Those clocks—"

"Twelve of them for fifty bucks at the auction," I told him proudly. "I'm selling them for nine ninety-five."

"Not bad," he admitted, "but that hearse outside with Ebbtide Shop painted on the side—"

"Not a hearse, Mr. Georgerakis, a van."

"It could bury you from what it must have cost. Watch out or I'll charge you twelve dollars a day for my services. Where's the old jukebox?"

He whistled faintly when I told him the price I'd gotten for it. We shared a cup of coffee and then he patted my hand and said the shop looked just like me, sunny and bright and cheerful. Since I'd just climbed out of the black hole of Calcutta I was inordinately pleased by the compliment.

"See you tomorrow at eight," he said. "It will be a pleasure."

Tomorrow at eight ... I remembered what that meant— Portland, Maine—and nearly panicked. I had to reread moment you lost consciousness and fell. The bullet hit Tuttle at the bottom of the stairs instead, whereupon he fell over and you landed on top of him. Which is where you were when I smashed down the door and found you."

How very complicated life sounded, I thought, and how very fast Joe talked. "Weird," I said politely, for it had no reality for me now. "I hope no one was hurt." I was still half clinging to the maze, willing it to come back to me so that I could discover what lay at the end of it. But Joe was talking again, naming names that tugged at my other memory and willing me to listen to him instead.

"Tuttle's still alive," he was saying, "but Holton's dead. Holton went back up to the roof and killed himself there. Tuttle's been arraigned as an accessory to your near-murder and he's in all the newspapers but no longer smiling. The police know about Hannah now, too. Robin and I took them all the papers and documents."

"Ah," I said, nodding at the name Hannah, and wondered if it had been she who guided me through the maze. I said drowsily, "I love you, too, Joe, but I couldn't find you. When I got home."

I didn't understand why he looked as if he were going to explode; he looked the same way he'd looked when I told him I had to go to Maine to find Hannah. I watched in wonder as he swallowed his anger, I could see him literally bite it off and swallow it.

He said in a ludicrously controlled, even voice, "I spent two days in Maine looking for you, Amelia. *Two days.*"

"But you *left* Maine," I said, frowning.

"I went *back* to Maine," he said. "I phoned you on Tuesday night at the Golden Kingfisher Motel, Amelia. Tuesday *night*. You weren't there. You weren't there

217

at midnight or at half-past midnight or at one o'clock in the morning, or at two. The manager found your suitcase there, but not you *or* the van."

"Weird," I said, watching him and thinking he had lovely eyes.

"Weird!" he echoed in a strangled voice. "As soon as I finished in court on Wednesday I hopped the first plane and by two o'clock in the afternoon I was back in Anglesworth with the state police."

I stared at him in amazement.

"I will not," he said, seeing that he had my full attention at last, "go into my reactions when I learned that Hannah's house had burned to the ground, or that the tire marks of a medium-sized van were found nearby in the grass. I will only tell you that it was twenty-four more hours before I knew that you were still alive. That's when the state police finally traced your van to a place called the Bide-a-Wee motel where a girl answering your description registered at ten o'clock soaking wet, and checked out several hours later. And then, Amelia—my God, Amelia, I barely got back in time."

"Back?" I repeated blurredly. It seemed a very long story that Joe insisted I hear.

"To Trafton, to find your telegram on my doorstep. In time to rush to your shop and find you lying with Tuttle at the bottom of the stairs. In time to prevent Holton from shooting you again."

I said clearly and firmly, "They were Despas, Joe, and Nora was one of them, I learned that. But I'm not."

"Amelia," Joe said patiently, "you *are* going to marry me, aren't you?"

"Well," I began, and then hesitated. Perhaps, I thought, I had found the heart of the maze after all. Right here. Now. In this room. Me. But without finishing either my sentence or my thought I fell asleep, and the next day Joe had to repeat everything he'd said to me all over again.

And so it became just one more sordid story that would titillate newspaper readers all through the fall and winter of the trial. A slightly demented Horatio Alger story of a clever young man who years ago learned to use a handsome face and a broad smile—twelve teeth showing, after all—to charm his way into Hannah's family and destroy it. And an older man, frustrated, pedantic, ambitious, who was looking for just such a young man with a big smile to exploit for his own purposes, for of what use is a handsome face and a broad smile—or ambition and knowledge—without power? And money is power. And Hannah had money.

And they got away with it, like the old-time marauders who sacked villages at night, leaving blood in their wake, except they wore business suits and ties, and they smiled a lot and covered everything up, including their real faces.

The one thing they never dreamed of in their wildest moments was Hannah's note. Or my curiosity, for that matter.

This pleases me. The little things still count.

In the tabloids Hannah was barely mentioned at all, but the New York *Times* reprinted their long-ago review of *The Maze in the Heart of the Castle,* and the book is going to be reissued at the same time that *In the Land of the Golden Warriors* will be published. For the latter book Robin has been asked to write a Foreword, and in it he is explaining the circumstances of the manuscript's discovery, and he is dedicating the book to me because Hannah would have wanted it, he says.

Neither will bring Hannah back to life, of course. Or

will they? Just a little? If she was a ghost I think she has been laid to rest now, although at times I still feel very close to her.

I think now about how our lives all touch each other, gently or violently, for good or evil, as Hannah's life touched mine. People's futures have been rearranged by all this. Robin, for instance, is going to have money again, enough so that he needn't dye his hair and climb five flights of stairs to sleep. It's too late for Hannah's will to be upset but a very good lawyer advised him to sue the senator for damages, and when this became evident there was a hasty and very large settlement out of court to avoid even more publicity.

As for Nora, she is dead. Robin tells me that she died of heart failure at what he believes to be the precise moment that Jay Tuttle was shot on the stairs. As if she knew. I think about this sometimes. . . . The newspapers carried photos of Tuttle's heiress wife, daughter of the famous Senator Plumtree—such a very suitable combination for Holton's wildest dreams—and yet I wonder. . . . Tuttle chose to keep Nora alive and in luxury for years, refusing to allow Holton to kill her, perhaps the only time he ever stood up to Holton; he visited her surprisingly often, too, for such a busy man. There are curious bonds between people of love and guilt and pity and remorse, and who is to say that Nora and Jay hadn't gone on loving each other all those years? Often I wonder what their lives might have been if Tuttle had been less malleable and Holton less ambitious. I blame Hubert Holton for much more than murder.

From Garwin Mason there came flowers: the news of Tuttle's fall from grace must have been very big in Maine. There was no note enclosed, only his name on a card, but there was no need for a note, I knew what he wanted to say.

The affair touched even Daisy, or Doris Tucci, who

surprised me very much by coming to see me in the hospital. She brought me flowers and also, with a grin, a hairbrush. She shook her head over me and told me I was a damn fool, and lucky to be alive.

"I know," I said meekly, thinking that Daisy had a very broad maternal streak in her. "You told me I was a nut."

"Like a fruitcake," she said, nodding. "The newspapers didn't explain too clearly why this senator and his aide felt they had to kill you, but I got the point, seeing how I was in on the beginning of it."

"Yes you were," I said wonderingly, "and if you hadn't told me—"

"If I hadn't, you wouldn't be lying here," she pointed out, "but also that sexy senator and his pal would still be on the loose, wouldn't they? Well, kid—" She reserved her liveliest bombshell for departure, announcing at the door with an impish grin, "Ollie and I got married yesterday."

I sat up in astonishment. "Daisy! *Married?* Congratulations!"

"Yeah," she said, nodding. "I owe you for that. Obviously a million bucks attracts leeches and vultures which a person needs like a hole in the head. So stop in sometime and watch me burp babies and do the domestic, okay?"

From the small sounds that reached me from the corridor as she left I guessed that her departure did not go unnoticed by doctors, interns, patients, and visitors.

As for myself, now that my excursion into violence is over, I feel changed in a way that is not explainable except, perhaps, to say that I have moved from Victim to Survivor, a distance of no small import. Some things matter more to me now, and many things less, and the past not at all. A balance has occurred that astonishes me: I am turning into a very agile tightrope walker, gliding across chasms and abysses without a glance below. I have no more nightmares and, ironically, now that I have come so very near to death it no longer haunts me. Joe says I am moving from Old Age to Middle Age and he suggests we get married in time for my Adolescence.

Amman Singh says that I have begun to walk the path to my Original Self. When I smile and ask him why he only quotes a proverb to the effect that no one can learn to live who has not learned to die.

What Dr. Merivale would say is something else again. As a matter of fact I met him just the other day on Main Street. He looked very trim, very well-groomed in his business suit, his face deeply tanned, which reminded me that May was always his vacation month, when he flew south to the Caribbean.

I said, "Hello there, Dr. Merivale!"

He stopped and looked at me, surprised. "Why—it's Amelia, isn't it?"

I'd forgotten how vague he could be; he'd always been nondirective as a psychiatrist and I suppose this enters subtly into the personality. He said, focusing on me reproachfully, "I'm sorry you've not come back for more treatment, Amelia, I feel your father would have wanted that. What have you been doing since I last saw you?"

I like Dr. Merivale, I really do. I mean, he held my hand for three difficult years and I am grateful for this but I was feeling mischievous that day. He had been away, of course, and so he'd not seen the newspapers, or the photograph of me being carried out on a stretcher from the Ebbtide Shop, with Joe in hot pursuit. I said gravely, "Well, Dr. Merivale, since I last saw you I've been looking for the murderers of a woman killed many years ago. I found them and was nearly murdered myself, and now one killer is dead and the other arrested. I've found a guru of sorts, I've fallen in love, and I've lost my virginity. I really think I've been Affecting My Environment, don't you? At last?"

It's possible that the passing of a truck blurred my words, or it's possible that Dr. Merivale is not by nature playful. His glance at me sharpened suspiciously and then retreated in haste. "Ah," he murmured, nodding. "Mmmm . . . well, I hope you will still consider that typing class, Amelia. It's so important—as I've stressed before—that we all have purpose in life." And having said this he gave me a kindly smile and continued walking down the street.

I stood and watched him go, and I laughed. I mean, have you ever stopped to realize—not just the miracle that life is—but how basically comic it is despite its griefs? The wonder of it, as Amman Singh says, is that we take it so seriously.

One day, poised on my tightrope, I hope to manage a glorious cartwheel, or at the very least a pirouette.

In the meantime, however, I bought a flower from the vendor on the corner and carried it home to Joe.

Discover—or rediscover—Dorothy Gilman's feisty grandmother and fearless CIA agent . . . Mrs. Pollifax!

THE UNEXPECTED MRS. POLLIFAX
THE AMAZING MRS. POLLIFAX
THE ELUSIVE MRS. POLLIFAX
A PALM FOR MRS. POLLIFAX
MRS. POLLIFAX ON SAFARI
MRS. POLLIFAX ON THE CHINA STATION
MRS. POLLIFAX AND THE HONG KONG BUDDHA
MRS. POLLIFAX AND THE GOLDEN TRIANGLE
MRS. POLLIFAX AND THE WHIRLING DERVISH
MRS. POLLIFAX AND THE SECOND THIEF
MRS. POLLIFAX PURSUED
MRS. POLLIFAX AND THE LION KILLER

Published by Fawcett Books.
Available wherever books are sold.